You Said She's Where?

You Said She's Where?

Sue Webb

Copyright © 2025 Sue Webb

The moral right of the author has been asserted.

Apart from any fair dealing for the purposes of research or private study,
or criticism or review, as permitted under the Copyright, Designs and Patents
Act 1988, this publication may only be reproduced, stored or transmitted, in
any form or by any means, with the prior permission in writing of the
publishers, or in the case of reprographic reproduction in accordance with
the terms of licences issued by the Copyright Licensing Agency. Enquiries
concerning reproduction outside those terms should be sent to the publishers.

The manufacturer's authorised representative in the EU for product safety is Authorised Rep
Compliance Ltd, 71 Lower Baggot Street, Dublin D02 P593 Ireland
(www.arccompliance.com)

This is a work of fiction. Names, characters, businesses, places, events
and incidents are either the products of the author's imagination
or used in a fictitious manner. Any resemblance to actual persons,
living or dead, or actual events is purely coincidental.

Troubador Publishing Ltd
Unit E2 Airfield Business Park,
Harrison Road, Market Harborough,
Leicestershire LE16 7UL
Tel: 0116 279 2299
Email: books@troubador.co.uk
Web: www.troubador.co.uk

ISBN 978-1-83628-267-9

British Library Cataloguing in Publication Data.
A catalogue record for this book is available from the British Library.

Printed and bound in Great Britain by 4edge Limited
Typeset in 11pt Minion Pro by Troubador Publishing Ltd, Leicester, UK

For Margaret

Prologue

Well, why not here? All along they'd threatened something like this. Why not in the place she'd taken for ultimate safety?

All she could see was a corner of the ceiling and part of two walls. She'd been lashed down in the tilting chair by her bedroom desk and tipped back. The posture of someone at the dentist: prone, passive, every thought trying to focus somewhere else.

They hadn't been hasty or nervous; so far no one had shouted at her. They'd even left her on her own for the time being while they strolled off elsewhere in the large, quiet house. A lavatory flushed downstairs, and twice there was the sound of a tap being run. She lay still, listening as if with every sense. In the kitchen the radio came to life; one of them was changing programmes back and forth.

The most everyday noises seemed significant now. She heard the clunk of the fridge door closing. They wanted her to wait, to feel that time was on their side, to sense the weight of not knowing what would happen next.

The familiarity of the comfortable room appalled her. It had been at the heart of her life as a cherished small child, then as a cheerful teenager. How could this be the same place – now, here, where she was being made to half sit, half lie, nearly immobile. She could scarcely believe the world beyond was going on unchanged. A blackbird flung out his rapturous song from the fig tree outside her window. Half a mile overhead, an airliner was passing, indifferent to where its shadow flitted across the city. All those years in and out of this room, being happy and free – with this, for her, as its final use?

Don't think about any of them – the people you've loved. It'll only make you weep. Whatever you do, don't let either of them see that.

At first, when they'd seized her and she'd fought back, all she'd felt was unreckoning rage. The sort that filled you with senseless energy and made you exclaim whatever came into your head. They had no right, was the thought that had kept repeating itself.

A swell of fear came next. They'd come in here literally barefaced: that was what frightened her. How could she be meant to live, if they hadn't bothered to put a blindfold on her? Or at least acted out the dark farce of wearing a hood?

But the worst thing, once they'd brought her in here, had been the ordinary briskness with which they went about their business. They might have been a couple of proctologists about to discuss their golf handicap over an exposed bowel. The only lapse into self-consciousness was when the younger one, taking out a gun, had needlessly shifted it to a different pocket. Evidently he couldn't bear for it not to be seen, just once.

When the hypodermic had come into view, all she could think of was trying not to piss herself.

If only they hadn't gone on to describe what it held. In her mind's eye she'd imagined the symptoms described in her own handwriting, as if her lecture notes were open in front of her.

Was that them now, coming up the basement stairs from the kitchen? Lurching her head to one side, she vomited up a gush of clear smelly fluid all down her right arm.

She couldn't believe this would be over quickly. All the signs were that they'd treat themselves to making her wait.

More terrible than any uncertainty was what she already knew about these men. Whatever they did to her, she wouldn't be the first.

That, surely, was what put them so triumphantly at their ease. The thing they said they'd do, she knew – she knew – at least one of them had done before.

And yes. Now they were coming back.

One

Nothing matters to me more than this.

Miranda had to tell herself so quite often. This was the year her class had graduated from clinical medicine to seeing real patients and so far every day thrilled her.

But now that they were out on the wards, what an incongruous sight they must be. Around them every sort of person wheezed or muttered, or struggled not to be wrong-footed by death, while she and the other students were all shining health and privileged innocence. Until the first day they'd entered St Edmund's, most of them had been spared everything and denied nothing; she knew she had. They even averaged a couple of inches taller than most people their age. What could any of them know to put even a speckle of iron in the soul?

'People in this country average fifty-two years of age,' so the Dean had said in his introductory lecture, 'before they encounter their first corpse.'

Today's ward round was being made by Mr Jameson, consultant physician. In attendance were a registrar, senior house officer, houseman and deputy matron. Half a step behind them the rest of the group were students, clad in too-new short white jackets. They formed a silent chorus silhouetted in a blast of sunlight through the ward's long windows. In distant St Mary Axe the half-built Gherkin, overtopped by cranes, was an ugly dense protrusion within a rising tide of glass.

'...The condition doesn't seem idiopathic,' the first patient was saying. She looked up at them all as one of the students tried to palpate her upper abdomen: Miranda's friend Frances, nervously unaware that she was still holding an open book under one arm.

'At least, I think I know what caused it.' The patient was about forty, with a shrewd, open face, and looked as if she relished dropping a clue to her condition. The deputy matron glanced warily at Mr Jameson, fearing this might be someone with a medical vocabulary of half a dozen words who was determined to show off each one.

In fact the patient was somebody senior from the Royal College of Nursing, who knew perfectly well when it made sense to say nothing. She was also considerate enough not to react at the fumbling diagnosis given by poor, clever Frances, whose anxious sympathy with others' sufferings could be quite at odds with the air of reassurance most patients wanted.

'Well, there's something there,' Frances ventured. 'Between the chest and the upper abdomen.'

'"Something"?' Mr Jameson gave her the full brunt of his attention. Physically he looked what he was: a recently fearsome quarter-back, the scourge of other hospitals' rugger teams. People who didn't know him found his meaty, squared-off appearance at odds with the meticulous self he showed at work.

Frances blushed right down to her waist. She was as tall as Mr Jameson and unfailingly neat, the sort who ironed her underwear. During the first two years at St Edmund's she'd come top in everything. Down in the dissecting room from the start she'd been no more likely than the Professor of Anatomy himself to confuse a femoral artery with your common iliac; and after the first few days no lecturer could ask her a question without everyone registering an expectant tremor.

No longer was their life mostly lectures. Sure, there'd been nothing very demanding about cutting up cadavers; it had found them busy and happy as kids with a new set of Lego. But now all those peaceable corpses were succeeded by actual suffering fellow-creatures, some of them quite vocal. This was where a lot of people got excited – and a bit relieved – to find anatomy enthralled them after all. Suddenly their training had perspective. But kind-hearted Frances wasn't coping. It had taken her until now to discover just how fazed she was by real illness rather than the kind you saw in diagrams.

She said, as loudly as she dared, 'A protrusion of some sort? 'A growth?'

'And the other symptoms?' Mr Jameson gave her a rock-steady look. He was a courteous and kindly man. Even so, people watched themselves around him. Right now he seemed to Frances like a worst-case diagnosis personified.

'Anyone? – No, not you, Miranda.'

Thomas St Clair spoke up. He was a handsome fair-haired man, five or six years older than the rest of them, and when Miranda reached his age this was how she'd like to be. Anyone could be fearless in the face of some terrible or embarrassing condition, if they were unfeeling enough. Thomas radiated confidence all right, but with the look of someone who could identify with the patient.

'The symptoms shown by Mrs Aubertin included pallor, fatigue, pain behind the lower end of the breastbone, vomiting, and difficulty in swallowing.' Some of the more promising students noticed his use of the woman's name rather than 'the patient in bed five here'.

Before Thomas could give a diagnosis Jameson turned to Frances. 'And what do we deduce from this?'

She decided to go for it, as if not caring who might overhear.

'Cancer? Of the stomach? Stomach cancer? I mean…' Jameson showed nothing. 'Thomas?'

Thomas looked past Jameson, straight at the patient, as though he and she were the only people there. 'There certainly is a new growth. And the stomach is definitely the affected organ.'

Several people avoided the woman's eye. Those who didn't, saw her show nothing more than good-natured interest.

'Anyone else?' Jameson asked.

Miranda was eight years old again, hand up in class, pleading to be asked. In response to a nod of acknowledgement she said, 'I think Mrs Aubertin shows the symptoms of two conditions. I believe she gave birth earlier this month, which might explain the tiredness and pallor.' She was chancing it, but there was no ignoring the sense of being smack on target. Yesterday she'd glimpsed a visiting husband lead a toddler up to this bed. Strapped to his front, as if gestating for a second time, an infant had lolled in the vacant sleep of the new-born.

'Also, in spite of the symptoms just mentioned, Mrs Aubertin's appetite is good.' This happened to be Nursing Week, when the third-years helped out on the wards, the better to know how the whole place was held together by the nursing staff. While improvising hand signals with a partial stroke victim nearby, Miranda had seen this patient happily put away an extended breakfast of porridge, scrambled egg, cereal and extra toast, with two sugared cups of tea.

'I would guess – I mean, my opinion is – that she has a hiatus hernia, possibly provoked by abdominal pressure on the diaphragm during pregnancy.'

The patient gave a cheerful yes-of-course sort of smile that made Miranda's whole week. Mr Jameson, though, did little more than agree. If he was never rude to junior staff, he was just as unlikely to be effusive.

Later, when they were crowded into the privacy of his office, he was more forthcoming.

'It is never acceptable,' he insisted, 'to say "or something" when offering a diagnosis. Or to hedge about and be vague – any more than you'd look competent when biting your nails or clearing out earwax with your little finger. Also the word "cancer" is never used in a patient's hearing when avoidable. Any other substitutes apart from "new growth"? – yes? – Frances?'

'Mitotic lesion; neoplasm? … ' It was like Mr Jameson to let her show how much she really did know.

Sometimes this place still terrified Miranda. And every day she couldn't get enough of it. In at least one more way they now had to measure up to the other staff, from the Dean to the orderlies. It was a new sensation, not looking flustered whenever it was her turn to inflict some intimacy on a sick stranger. But she was damned if she wasn't going to grow up and cope. She didn't just owe it to herself – that went for everyone here – but to so many others. To her mother above all. She knew – and was grateful for it – how Laura had acted with patients of her own. Steadfast if need be from first diagnosis through to eternity.

Some memories Miranda called up a lot.

'Of course you're up to it, you silly sausage.' This, when Miranda had got her place in med school. 'Coping with things is what you do best.'

Laura had always been careful to say things like that; so was Adam. When Miranda recalled how her parents used to be, her mind's eye showed them with an arm round each other's waist, looking at herself or little Josh with a shared expression of pride. 'Like a king and queen together on one coin,' she'd once told them when she was seven.

Everyone was bound to think she'd been influenced by Laura, choosing medicine. It wasn't entirely true.

'Why,' someone had asked at the admissions interview, 'do you think so many medical students are the children of doctors?' They'd automatically offered to see Miranda, as a courtesy shown to any candidate whose parent had graduated from St Edmund's. It wasn't that Laura had gone on to be anybody grand. But as an inner-city GP she'd been famous across thirty square miles of London as someone who did small things well. Miranda and her brother had still been little when they'd sensed her status in the local practice. As they waited in their school uniforms for a lift home, trying not to fidget, the two receptionists would treat them as respectfully as if they'd been trainee royalty. And whenever a Turkish pensioner or an overstretched teenage mother rang in, it was always Laura they put out for. 'I'm sorry, she's got no appointments free,' was one of the first phrases Josh had learned to burble down his toy telephone, followed by his rendering of 'Is there another doctor you'd like to see?' One elderly Calabrian lady used to ask, 'Please can I see Mrs Big Smile?'

And how else did Miranda remember her mother? If anyone had asked what was the highest praise she could offer, she'd probably have said, 'My mother was just my mother. What else should she have been?'

'But that's my job,' Laura had once told her, laughing off some such affectionate comment. 'I have to be here, always the same. How else can you learn to ignore me?'

In the interview Miranda had told them, 'I've no idea why medicine runs in families. It was always what I'd hoped for, long before noticing what my mother did. All I can say is, if you want something badly enough, you may not bother to ask the reason why.'

Two

It had been a perfect childhood. Privileged, too, unlike many on that side of town.

In every big city, one neighbourhood is marked 'Arrivals'. The best place on earth, you'd think. Enough people have struggled to reach it from far away.

Round Albany Square lies part of London that houses them all: Cypriot enforcers and dreadlocked social workers; sparrow-like men from the Bangladeshi floodlands, with large families rarely seen on the street. Scruffy young Queenslanders wearing good health like a flag of nationhood. It's Noah's ark for humans.

Outsiders mistake this side of town, thinking only of dinginess and dole. In fact a ragged coastline of prosperity runs right through it. On scores of Victorian streets, one side of the party wall can be a maze of bed-sits, flimsy as voting booths. In the family home next door it's all restored cornices and spacious gentility. So too when you look outwards, east of Churchyard Walk Wine Bar and the Good Earth vegetarian restaurant; past the Irish Women's advice centre, the Caribbean takeaway, and the lesbian health club making the best of it in silver masonry paint like a DIY Christmas decoration. Even beyond the municipal park round a former country house there are islands of well-being, each more remote as you go towards the reservoirs and marshalling yards and the distant pre-war suburbs.

Albany Square was one such outpost, where throughout their childhood nothing had threatened to change. So it felt strange to find the house deserted one day as everyone from her flat-share followed Miranda upstairs.

'This place is nothing but a funhouse!'

So said Alicia's boyfriend Richard, as they trooped into what had been Miranda's bed-sitting room. They'd come to help move out some of her stuff, including the music centre, a recent birthday present from Adam. His gift had been late; understandably, perhaps, so soon after all the heart-wrenched busyness around Laura's funeral. But it still was unthinkingly generous; as usual her father had been indulging himself as well as her, in spending so much and choosing so carefully.

The speakers, though, had been commissioned for precisely this size of room – presumably as an oversight, since Miranda had already left home. Could it have been an involuntary resistance to the thought of getting older in an emptying house? She and Adam had said almost nothing to each other about Laura's death. The fact of losing her was like a sudden alien visitation, to be tiptoed around and sized up with extreme care.

Many homes have their own special purpose. Some are designed for partying, in one large hard-to-heat space. Others are stuffed with zealously dusted knick-knacks announcing pride of possession. What this house had advertised was childhood. It was a shrine to every stage of infancy, from the nursery-school doodles framed in the hallway to a much-loved rocking horse put out to retirement in one of the drawing-room windows.

On the first-floor landing a wall of snapshots under glass spanned most of their family's life. Josh, a toddler off to a fancy-dress party, all solemn pride in his home-made costume. Adam, rehearsing a playlet written for Miranda's sixth birthday, was spreadeagled as the bag in a big game hunt while his children each delightedly placed a foot on him. In a snow-dredged garden all of them were hot and happy around Josh's first snowman, dressed in a dusty mortarboard and a kipper tie.

If any picture recurred, it was Miranda's parents together. As often as not, they faced the camera while smiling in each other's arms. You could see from their shared expression that such photos were taken by a child – especially the early pictures, badly exposed and taken by someone obviously two feet tall, so that Laura and Adam dwindled way up into the sky. In memory they often seemed to have been laughing together, or else Adam was making Laura hoot with merriment till she could hardly breathe. He'd lifted her spirits and made her forget herself; she'd anchored him and gave him a sense of who he was and what he might yet be...

'Hey, Allie, how about that!' said Richard, straining to examine a snap of the family at a kite festival, blithely classless on Hackney Marshes. He and sexy Alicia were draped around each other as if born conjoined.

Alicia's own calm enthusiasm was directed at Miranda's bedroom. 'Now those are really not bad.' She was looking at a two-hundred-year-old pier glass and a Regency bed, both another example of Adam splurging on impulse for the pleasure of giving a surprise. At eight years old Miranda could easily have been too young to appreciate them. As it was, she'd known just enough history to be thrilled – noisily, boringly so, she suspected – by picturing the hard-to-believe appearance of the people who would have used them first.

'This wasn't done by you.' Jeanette, who Miranda had known since school, was marvelling at a mural that covered the largest wall inside one bedroom. It showed Adam and Laura peering round a trompe l'oeil door, aghast at a meticulously rendered Himalaya of dirty clothes and neglected homework. 'It must be one of your brother's paintings.'

'He was fourteen when he did that.' Miranda found herself feeling more like a proud parent than just an elder sister. Maddeningly, without warning, her eyes prickled with tears at the thought of how different he'd been then. Poor Joshie...

'This was a good likeness,' Jeanette quickly remarked, in her mild contralto. She was a RADA graduate, of whom hopeful things were said. She went forward the better to scrutinize Laura's picture. Miranda's mother had been dark-haired, with a colouring that showed rude health to its best advantage. 'It could be you, thirty-something years on.'

'It is just like her. And I do hope so.'

Josh's best effort had been made for the drawing room. Some months before, Laura had sat to him for a portrait to hang in pride of place. If the mural upstairs was more than an accomplished cartoon, this painting also defied expectations, with none of the vapid elegance you often see bestowed on people's wives. 'What on earth were you both talking about?' was something he'd been asked more than once.

But the picture wasn't there. Only a pale rectangle on the sprigged wallpaper showed where its usual place had been.

A glance round the room showed what had become of it. Laura and her expression of calm good cheer had been taken down and slid behind the biggest sofa, sideways in the dusty gloom where Josh and Miranda used to be discouraged from leaving chocolate wrappers and apple cores.

'I wonder where Adam's moving it to,' Miranda felt obliged to say.

'Perhaps he doesn't want to be reminded. I mean, till later.' Jeanette made a point of speaking lightly.

Miranda took in the rest of the familiar room. At first with a twitch of surprise; then with hot bewilderment.

Much of the furniture was missing, so that the place looked like a Harley Street waiting room, expensive but bleak. The smaller stuff had all been put away to make more space. Not only did this not look like a house of mourning: it was readying itself for a party. Crates of glasses and a portable fridge stood in one corner, and out beyond the French windows a partly-constructed marquee sheltered stacks of portable chairs. In front of both marble fireplaces a stook of red roses thickened the air with their scent.

The space left by Laura's portrait wasn't entirely empty. Propped against it, a pale-blue teddy bear stuck its giant furry soles several inches out from the mantelpiece. The pink satin bow around its neck could have gift-wrapped a five-hundred-pound grizzly.

*

Back at the flat Miranda was glad to be phoning from somewhere private. For some reason the call to Adam's office wasn't following its usual easy course. After she'd asked his PA how her children were, instead of sharing a couple of minutes' chat Wendy just gave a quick, faintly embarrassed, 'Very well, thank you.' A tiny pause followed before Miranda realised she wasn't going say anything more; this was a call that Wendy was somehow anxious to deal with swiftly. Sounding both brisk and uncertain, she said, 'I'll see if Adam's in.'

A silence followed. It lasted two minutes.

'Darling!' Adam's voice was determinedly cheerful. 'You're well, I trust?'

Before she knew it, Miranda found herself saying splendid thank you in similar ho-ho fashion. She was amazed. Could this be one more of the bizarre ways that grief can show itself? Was she really supposed to accept that she and her own father were jollying each other up like a couple of useful acquaintances at a party?

'Thanks for my present. It's wonderful. And the speakers balance out beautifully—'

'The what…? God, yes, of course. So you went to the house…?'

Some impulse made her try and help him off the hook. 'Dad, I'm glad you're up to partying.'

She realized neither of them was going to mention Laura by name. What had made it worse was that there'd been no time to prepare for her loss. An instant had been all it took to fling her mother away, through her windscreen onto a rain-soused slip road and out of this world.

'So you saw all that.'

She waited. God knows what reassurances she'd hoped for. But she hadn't expected her father to sound evasive.

'Uh – extraordinary teddy.' What she most desired and feared to know about was the floral arrangement propped on the drawing room mantelpiece. With a wording of pink and white blooms against a background of red carnations, in the shape of a heart.

'Oh, right.' She pictured him rallying himself, as if, routinely resolute, he was straightening out some stiff libel suit or a dispute with a print union. Adam's working life featured several worlds. As well as a newspaperman he was also an economist, grand enough for any number of quangos and consultancies. With his combined straightforwardness and tact, it had always seemed there was no situation he couldn't handle.

She hadn't expected to be one of them.

'Mandy, there's something I've wanted to tell you.'

'Oh?'

You Said She's Where?

'I expect you saw the decoration and so forth?'

'Uh, yes?'

'Well, it concerns – how can I do this justice – someone who's anxious – no, who I'm sure will be delighted – thrilled, indeed – to get to know you better.'

'Better?'

'I'm sorry – maybe I didn't put that quite right. I mean, someone who would like to meet you – in a few days now – and get to know you, more than anything in the world. And need I say, it would make me supremely happy.'

Three

In the floral centrepiece of the Albany Square drawing room, 'Julie and Adam' had been the declaration wrought in densely wired blooms, the down-stroke of her J running into the leading edge of his A. Her idea, not his. And definitely nothing to do with Julie St Clair's mother, Etta, whose energy and initiative had no equal in the cause of getting things right.

Etta was bent on this now, as she readied herself for work.

'If you want to surprise Adam in future, leave it to me, won't you? Whenever it's something other people might see.' Privately Etta thought Adam himself had been led into ultimate naffness with his gift of the blue teddy bear.

'From now on, doing such things properly is the least one owes him. As a top man in his field.' Etta was standing even straighter than usual as she said this, full of the sap of rising professional hopes. Hard upon her election to the borough council she'd been moving with a late starter's singleness of purpose towards selection as a parliamentary candidate.

It was murmured nowadays at party headquarters that

her main purpose on this earth was to act as host animal to an array of power suits. One of these, in black and yellow, was making a forthright statement about her now as she crisped up her hair for the day with precision bursts of lacquer. On the sofa meanwhile, Julie embodied the very principle of passivity.

'Have I really got to get something new for this party? Adam says he likes me whatever I wear.'

'Of course you must,' said Etta calmly. 'For an engagement party.'

Julie sighed. If there was one thing she really hated, it was having to make her mind up.

'You could wear your black mini-dress. If one accessorized it properly.'

'It's got stuff on it.' Julie didn't say if she meant Thousand Island dressing, spunk or Babycham.

'That was weeks ago! In all that time have you seriously not taken your good dress to be cleaned?'

Julie gave an unresentful twitch of exasperation at her own laziness. She had the presence of mind not to defend the rest of her kaleidoscopically changeable wardrobe, from the sleeveless pink angora to the trouser outfit in silver paper. Today her hair, an infantine shade of blonde, jutted upwards in a pert off-side ponytail. It should have been a mistake, but wasn't. Her sweater looked misleadingly like a male cast-off, with its sleeves down to her translucent fingertips. By its contrast with Julie's winter-sunlight prettiness, grunge flattered her.

'I hope I'm not supposed to look old as well as posh. Like some people there.' Only six months had passed since she and Adam had first met, at an annual Open House given in Blackheath by the Dean of St Edmund's Hospital. She'd been squired by her brother Thomas, invited as one of the few most favoured students of his year. Her mother noted with frustration how she still seemed to be marrying just the man himself, without a thought for the world that came with him.

'Adam's friends? You mean Adam's friends and contacts?' Holding the spray can aloft, unconsciously flamenco, Etta cast a stare at her daughter's heavy black boots and spun-glass ankles. 'I've told you.' As she spoke, she punctuated herself with squirts from the can. 'Adam' – zap – 'is at the centre' – zap – 'of a lot of very caring and worthwhile people.'

As a politician she wasn't one to drop the jargon of social concern just because she was in private. These days even the family cat got addressed as though Etta was miked up.

*

Going to see her brother in the sick bay at his school, Miranda was stalked by ghosts. Too damned easy to be plucked at by memories, sitting on the train in a state of fugue. Mainly of Josh himself as he used to be.

'You're the worst singer in the universe!' he'd call out at their mother when, tunefully enough, she sang along at the wheel. Back then, aged nine, he'd worn a huge grin of affection when slagging off his family. At fifteen: 'Sorry, Dad, if you've wasted your time expecting trouble. But I can't be bothered with a difficult adolescence.' In Health Studies his teacher had said there must be something wrong with him if he never quarrelled with his parents. Bollocks, Josh had said afterwards. He'd been right too. It may have been uncommon, how he and his family got on, but that hadn't made it unreal.

There was no one else in the school sanatorium today. The place was silent apart from faint sports-field sounds and an expiring bluebottle on one of the windowsills. Her brother lay propped up in bed, staring out at the lush, nondescript view of sports fields and wooded multi-millionaire suburbia. A pair of headphones lay in his passive hands as though the sounds coming from them could seep in through his fingers. He didn't seem to notice her until she'd sat down by the bed.

At St Edmund's, bracing up each day against unfamiliar responsibilities, she'd never dare let down her guard and feel as heartsore as this. It had been the day before Laura's funeral, held on a blossoming day in April, all birdsong and milky sunlight, that Josh had been swept semi-conscious into hospital under an ambulance siren. Miranda too had gone sick next morning, waking to find the inside of her elbows crusted and raging from the unfamiliar symptoms of eczema.

Josh was long since out of danger, but he'd been left languid and serious by a hard convalescence. One that should have been spent at home.

'I'm glad it's you, Mandy.' He turned his thin face towards her. Since going sick he'd had a bleached-ivory look, emphasised by his dark hair.

Pneumonia oughtn't to be such a big deal as this. Not for her gifted brother, until now so cheerfully fearless in his world of good prospects. Caught short by how he still looked, she fell back on banter. 'I thought someone ought to make social demands on you. Who else has been?'

'My friends. By definition, you could say.'

She hoped in vain for a glint of irony. In recent weeks he'd become both younger – not innocent, but childish – and prematurely old. Mostly he seemed removed from the world in a way that made most people's concerns seem small if not downright silly.

'You could go home for a few days.' She still didn't know why, last term, he'd insisted so suddenly on becoming a boarder. There'd been no sign of him falling out with either of their parents.

Instead of answering, he said, 'And how about you? Over at the hospital.'

It wasn't like him to be polite, let alone evasive.

'Or you could stay in the flat – we've got room. And there's lots going on.'

'I couldn't bear lots going on. Thanks all the same.' He added in a brittle tone, as if resenting his own good manners, 'And don't be miserable because of me, Mandy.'

She looked away, towards the empty room with its two other perfectly made beds. The last pupil in here had only stayed a few hours: a kid from Middle School whose big toenail had been hit end on by a ball from a nearby cricket practice.

This time, there was one particular reason she was here. She couldn't not mention it.

'About Dad's new plans …'

'What about them, then?' He gave her a hard look.

She'd known exactly what she'd meant to say. Right up to, 'So we must try and be happy for him, and understand him as soon as we get the chance …' But her careful little speech refused to haul itself out of her mouth.

'I do know about it, you know.' His tone was contemptuous. That too was something she'd never heard before. 'He got Matron to tell me.' Josh went on staring at Miranda, as if their father's upcoming marriage was some incriminating deed of hers.

She made her speech anyway, or something like it.

'…at the worst, he might just be on the rebound.' She meant it for her own sake as much as for Josh. 'Maybe Dad's just crazy with rage at losing – at what he's just lost. At being bereaved…'

Chancing a look at him, she was silenced. His handsome features had soundlessly morphed into a mask of tears and snot.

'Joshie… Do you want me to leave you alone?'

He shook his head, which made it worse. What seventeen-year-old boy – debilitating illness be damned – didn't care if he was seen to cry?

'Is it something you want to talk about? Later – before I leave?'

Another shake of the head, violent and crooked, as if losing control of gesture as well as words.

She sat beside him in silence for a long time. Neither of them mentioned family again that day.

Four

Adam was exultant and dishevelled, from performing an act of worship on the body of his fiancée. He gazed at her now as she reclined on a cumulo-nimbus of pillows in a pose unwittingly classical. Self-conscious or not, Julie's graceful passivity was his new female ideal.

'Whom everything becomes. To chide, to laugh...' With a finger he caressed the contours inside the bend of her arm, full of solemnity at their perfection. She blushed, as always when he talked that way. From pleasure, so he thought; in fact from confusion. How was she supposed to know, half the time, if he wasn't quoting from something?

But an unpredictable childhood, with her mother alternating between nagging and neglect, had made Julie in some ways a quick study. Only a few months after she'd first known Adam really well, she was starting to see that ignorance itself might be adorable. It was a novelty for him to have a partner who knew so little of his world. Or who hung over him with a show of mystified anxiety each time he took his blood-pressure pills. It seemed the smallest thing about him could be new and dead brilliant.

So now, when he said, 'Tell me what's in your mind –

right now, while you're looking like that,' she didn't think for an instant of saying, 'Oh, nothing much.' Always be ready with something. That was what life with Etta had taught, even if Julie had never acknowledged it to herself.

She stretched, meeting his eyes with a look both lazy and demure. 'Remember our first time?' He liked her to ask that.

'I was just thinking the same thing!'

'You don't mind that I was hesitant?'

'I adore you for it. You don't mind that I wasn't?'

'You were adorable too. And while we were in there, all hidden, nobody else did come, did they?'

He laughed in conspiratorial delight at her unwitting pun and after a few moments so did she. Lapsed back on the pillow in parallel with her, he gazed at the ceiling in a trance of recollection… That steep climb to pure, top-note triumph as she seemed to want to hold him away from her…

'But I nearly came on you. Seeing the way you looked, right into my eyes.' Her face had been burnished blank of everything except surrender… 'You made me feel…'

'Divine?' That's what he'd said at the time.

'Yes – yes!' She'd looked as if he'd been an angel, he'd told her afterwards, with an upraised sword. And then. If this is like death, he'd thought, just as they say—

If this is death. Being extinguished. But still being. If this is it—

Still looking at the ceiling she said, 'Even before you touched me I was hurting there. I was like a huge new bruise.'

Struck into her rather, he thought. Like the executioner whose blow brought a prisoner's deliverance into martyrdom. She loved him all the more for that, she'd said. Hurting – just a bit – that was what made it even more real.

But was it her body that had taken possession of his? He hadn't known what being pleasured like that could do to the rest of sensation. The world around him didn't just fade down. It was gone; no other experience existed.

After the next time, in a hotel in Curzon Street, every expense relished by him, he'd felt reborn. And said so in the words of several poets.

She'd looked up at him with her water-nymph's hair tumbled across the pillow. 'You know, I really like it when you do that.'

'Do what?' he'd asked, bright with the certainty that her answer would please him.

'When you say things I haven't heard before. There's so much I'm going to learn that's new.'

*

It wasn't her ignorance itself that he cherished. What stirred him most was banishing it; in fragments, humbled each time at the gratitude that shone through her shy excitement.

Some things revealed an unexpected talent. Julie had somehow never owned a camera; her readily increasing deftness in composing and setting up video film surprised and delighted them both... When he thought she mightn't be looking, Adam cast a glance now, at a certain corner of the room.

He needn't have; her instinct for other people's desires and dislikes, hard won from infancy, had all that stuff well under control. Without anything said, she'd known that he'd hate it if whatever they'd just done together was allowed to run on and include any of the talking afterwards.

Well, she wasn't stupid, was she?

*

He can't see her as I do. No one like him could value her the way she deserves.

He only wanted her by chance, because she was there. He can't love her. What he really wants is being seen with her. She's always meant more than that to me.

I'm the one who takes in every detail of her. All the things he's too excited and distracted to look at. The other day, when she wore that waistcoat in a figured material. Each time she breathed, the pattern across her back slightly changed its shape. Someone in that room tried to pay her a compliment. I wish they wouldn't. They said she had skin like porcelain. All sorts of people tell her that.

Besides, her complexion isn't pink and white; it's rose and silver.

It's not her fault she's with him. She's always been ready to oblige other people's feelings. That's what I care for the most about her.

And through it all, he thinks he's being bold and free. Risking everything; living life off-piste, he once called it in some newspaper article. Blew the whistle on himself there. Hazard for rich dorks. It's not as if he hadn't still cared for the wife. Enough, at least, right at the start. And the whole world going on about his perfect family. Otherwise he'd never have come over so bright and moist at chancing all that.

Of course she'll come back to me. Of course she will. Till then I'll be the one – not him – who knows how to take it. How to be patient. I can wait.

But for now he's got some learning to do. Someone has to let him know what he's done. And I can show respect for justice better than he ever could.

I don't want him dead; safely out of it. I want him bereft. Feeling the way I do now.

Five

The Square had never been the family's only home. At weekends there'd been their own half of an eccentrically divided farmhouse – theirs, at least, by tacit understanding. The legal owner, who lived in the other part, was Laura's aunt Kitty. In their imaginations Miranda and her brother had always found it hard to separate Kitty and her home. Whenever she appeared in Albany Square, for birthdays or Christmas, it felt strange, as if the ghost of the farmhouse, its old barn and its little orchard, had somehow come with her.

Most Fridays Adam would be driven back early from Canada Wharf, to meet up with Josh and Miranda at Laura's surgery. In the quiet Islington street outside, the big Citroen would squat beneath a weight of weekend luggage packed the night before. Leaving the city, the horizons widening and growing clear, each change of programme on the car stereo marked a familiar stage of the journey. 'Pick of the Week is early; we're still on the Westway,' Adam would quip, as the throughway kept straightening before them like a fairground ride. An hour later, in heavy traffic up the last hill before the view of the

Weald, Josh and Miranda would ritually groan through the announcement of Any Questions. And shortly after nine they'd all chorus, 'Good evening to you, Alastair Cooke,' to mark being nearly there and leaving the Petworth road for a network of deep lanes.

In midsummer it was still daytime when they arrived at Stumblehurst Farm. Two miles across flood-prone meadows were the Downs, laid with blissful sweeps of light and shade. Beyond the No Through Road sign half hidden in cow parsley they'd dog-leg through the village and kill the engine amid stupefying riverbank quiet.

Now too this cherished place had changed, and receded from their life.

'I hadn't really thought how it would be, moving here.' Obediently lashed to a bleeper, Miranda's great-aunt looked doubly unfamiliar against her new well-ordered background of double-glazing and communal lawns.

'Actually it's not bad, being offered all this service. Like finding that you've somehow got a wife. Of the old-fashioned sort, I mean. Thanks – I can manage if you put the cup there.'

After a lifetime spent on more interesting things than her own comforts, Kitty planned to rent out the farmhouse to pay for sheltered accommodation and the nursing care that went with it. She was giving up her icy low-beamed bedroom, its bedstead made tolerable till now by stone hot-water bottles. The bare narrow stairs, crooked as a tornado, had also become too much. Hereafter her money would stretch, more or less, to central heating and that other novelty, regular meals. As an artist she had led a life of self-discipline, but only in her work. And even that had had to change in recent years, as the heavy labour of sculpting, in boiler suit and welder's mask, had had to go. These days Kitty only worked sitting down, designing lightscapes for public occasions amid the comfort of a huge swivel chair from which the starship Enterprise could have been piloted.

So here they were, drinking coffee by the open French window amid a residue of packing cases, like two stage hands taking a break on set. On the far side of the lawn a sprinkler was hissing. The view was older than the flat, dominated by trees in fashion with the Victorians: monkey puzzle, copper beech. A deep herbaceous border had been professionally planted out, beneath a high wall of soft-coloured brick and knapped flint. Seeing this decent-looking place, going on dignified, Miranda was reminded how uneasy she'd been at the thought of Kitty continuing to live alone.

The sight of Kitty herself was also a relief. In her worst imaginings she'd feared to find her aunt unmade at last by the effort of moving house, half collapsed maybe, like a botched Guy Fawkes in a go-cart. But though both knees were due for surgery, Kitty still looked easy and alert.

'I hope you'll get enough privacy,' Miranda said, pouring the coffee, 'living here.'

'Plenty of that, I'm glad to say.' Kitty was apt to remark that what others called loneliness, she saw as nothing worse than solitude.

Miranda took a gulp of mouth-crinkling strong

Arabica. Then another, almost too soon to avoid burning herself. *Go on, tell her. Before you've delayed so long that it's embarrassing.* She was aware of Kitty giving her a look of appraisal – steady but questing, just like Laura might have done. At least her aunt, with a spirit seasoned tough as oak, was unlikely to show distress at anything in what remained of her life.

So why, at every point, had she found a reason to keep Adam's news until later? A phone call would never have done – would it? Much better, surely, to say nothing until she and Kitty were face to face.

Besides she couldn't have said anything while the others were there. They'd driven down in two cars loaded with serious kit, hoping to spend that weekend jumping off Upping Beacon and gliding in the sunlit thermals of their hearts' desire. Apart from Jeanette they were mostly from the hospital's Para-gliding Society: Frances, Thomas, and Richard, with Alicia tagging along, and Jack, a guy just out of art school who was helping to restore some famous murals in the old part of St Edmund's. Everyone had briefly crowded into the room to say hello, borrow the keys to Kitty's half-emptied house, and look – quite shyly, some of them – at Miranda's aunt, rated internationally as an artist since before they were born. Against Kitty's purpose-built new home, with its ramps and fierce heating, their vivid health made them aliens, Technicolor characters infiltrating a movie made in black and white.

And after the others had left? Well, it would have been wrong to hurry through everything else there was to talk about. After half an hour had been gossiped away, there was finally a beat of silence. Miranda put down her mug, drew breath – and turned to hear Kitty say, 'I think you may have some news for me.'

'I do – I have.'

'Spit it out, then.' Before Miranda could answer, she added, 'I expect your father's getting married. He is, isn't he?'

'You knew that?'

'Josh mentioned something.' Kitty paused, then said, 'I don't think he'll take well to this new stepmother business... When is the wedding?'

Miranda told her. And was furious with herself for blushing at the closeness of the date. What was it to do with her that Adam was vowing a second time to forsake all others? She said, 'Perhaps Josh should meet her. Maybe if we all knew her – um, Julie, better – I mean, as more than just an idea...'

Kitty seemed to ignore this. She remarked, 'It's nobody's else's business, if he needs to grieve. No matter how long, poor young sod. Who knows how he'll be true to himself? Last time I saw him, the other month, he was right on that teenage cusp. Adult self-possession, only with "private, keep out" all over him like a solemn little boy. Hard to tell what kind of man he'd be.'

'Uncomfortable to know, perhaps,' Miranda said. 'A principled stickler, I mean. Almost certainly a better man than me.'

'I hope you're wrong – just a bit. Whatever sort of man or woman you plan to be. Sometimes a sense of justice can be rather disorderly. Breeds all sorts of dodgy deeds.

If he wants to get too angry with anyone, he could find the whole world against him.' Kitty spoke briskly, as if the idea was almost too familiar to be uttered aloud.

Dear Kitty, Miranda thought, you should know. I'll bet this isn't really about poor invalid Joshie, sick with rage at being bereaved. Isn't this your stroppy younger self you're describing? Not that it was easy to picture her aunt, whose looks had turned patrician with the years, as someone her own age, despite the familiar studio photographs of a young woman with a shoulder-length halo of dark hair. The nineteen-forties and their values seemed so distant, it took an effort of imagination to remember that World War II wasn't fought with longbows.

Indicating her temporarily crippled state, Kitty said, 'I shan't be seeing you at the wedding. In any case I prefer funerals. The person concerned is usually getting out of trouble rather than into it. But tell me about it, won't you.'

Six

The hearse was to be a thing of joy. Later that day its horses were due to enter Albany Square, at a stately prance with plumes tossing in the breeze and not one passer-by too busy to stare. Meanwhile they were being harnessed, in their breezeblock stable on the Hackney Marshes. Each gelding weighed three-quarters of a ton and shone like ancient polished oak. Whenever one of them moved, with the deliberateness of most powerful creatures, it was a public statue coming alive. This wasn't ordinary commerce; it was show business. The harness was saddle-soaped to the texture of soft old suede; the horses' oiled hooves gleamed, and their manes were plaited tight as flower-buds.

Buckling a crupper, the firm's senior member hoped to Christ the booking details were all right this time. When it came to knowing what contacts to work, his partner, who was also his brother, could be a clever little git. But sometimes he was a right stupid sod about checking over what he tried to let them in for. Like the time he'd been so full of that movie they were supposed to be in. Bloody lucky he'd only done the paperwork on that job and not the driving as well; it turned out the stupid bastards had wanted the hearse for a chase scene. Galloping over tarmac, for God's sake, with *their* horses – theirs, mind, not some expendable old nags provided by the film company. The two of them had nearly parted company over that one; but he was damned if he'd have his horses put at risk like that. They were the best there was for the job: a hundred percent traffic proof and pure black – not even a white sock between the pair of them. No proper funeral horse had white on its coat. Let alone scars left from falling down and breaking its knees, so the whole world knew you couldn't look out for your own animals. You wouldn't even have got by on carting successful villains to the boneyard; not looking like that.

*

Unknown to Miranda and her friends, while they were at the party their flat would not be empty.

Meanwhile the two intruders waited, parked at a careful distance just outside the street's only exit. They'd checked the place and knew there was building work in hand downstairs, with several other people in stained overalls to give them cover. The one in charge had left nothing unresearched: who lived here, what they looked like, what motors they drove. Plus he understood the sort of visitors you'd expect in this fashionable place: builders, caterers, interior decorators. At the house they were targeting, when a party was held by the people downstairs – curated, almost, like a must-see exhibition – its organizers were a

Knightsbridge firm owned by two brisk young ladies of title. And when any house on this terrace changed hands, it was usually the same removal firm who showed up, with their staff turned out in bowler hats. Fitting in would be no challenge; that was mainly why there were two of them, with their work-clothes and tool-bag. With both of them there it looked nearer the real thing. And more than one face made it harder for any witness to remember details.

*

Upstairs the flat-share was the usual scene of forced intimacy. Most weekends, there seemed to be people sleeping over on the floor and the morning after a party the bathroom readily featured some semi-stranger cleaning their teeth half naked while someone else took a dump.

What made this life okay was that everyone was young, healthy and transient; wherever each of them expected to live in a year or two it wasn't likely to be here.

'I wouldn't mind being late,' Miranda was saying, 'if, you know, Dad's er – if Julie was already a friend. Or at least someone I'd met. I've only seen her once, across a party somewhere.'

She and Jeanette were waiting for the bathroom, in a state of formal half-undress. Jeanette, barefoot and wearing an unfamiliar good suit, noted Miranda flipping her hands to and fro to dry a topcoat of nail varnish. She'd never gone to such lengths before.

'It's for you, not her,' said Jeanette, 'that you want to be on time. Whatshername – step-mama – wouldn't be hurt if you're late; but you'd feel ungracious as all hell. Has anyone told you your sense of decency is out of control?' Honesty, friendship's soundest coin. They'd known each other as children, then re-met at a hospital training session where Jeanette, newly post-RADA, was impersonating a difficult patient; and their alliance had re-established itself without missing a beat.

'Who's in there, anyway?' Miranda demanded. 'If it's Alicia, she's probably chosen this moment to give herself a total body transplant.'

'Go and bang on the door. If Richard's in there too, they know perfectly well the bathroom's a no-fuck zone.'

'I can't do that.'

'Why ever not?'

'If I snap at Alicia, next thing is that I'll say sorry. I'm damned if I want to find I've done that.'

Richard came out of the bathroom with a towel round his waist and started at the sight of them. Just like on stage. So people really did that.

He mumbled and vanished. Behind him Alicia sashayed out, in-your-face naked with a creamy expression.

'You'd better hurry,' she said. 'If we're not all going to be late.'

'I blame the jacuzzi for what goes on in there,' Jeanette said. She darted into the marble-lined bathroom. Amid chiaroscuro spot lighting an improbably large television was angled down from the ceiling. Instantly reappearing, she called out, 'You haven't even emptied it!'

Truly these were not the usual slum-linoleum student digs. In contrast with the cheerfully disordered lives led here, the flat itself showed no expense spared. It was the top floor of a house owned by Alicia's cousin, a theatrical agent who'd made his first couple of million aged twenty-eight. Downstairs the main drawing room was used mostly for parties and held almost nothing except modern art and a grand piano.

They scurried onto the street at last and contorted themselves into Miranda's litter-strewn Mini. Easing away and changing up, she had an unthinkable thought. For the first time in her life she didn't want to go back home.

Seven

The house was already full of guests and noise. Amid the scrum of sociability, at first sight the nearest thing to a familiar friend was Miranda's old rocking horse. It was dappled of course, an antique with real horsehair mane and tail. In recent years it had stood framed by tasselled drapes where it could overlook the Square.

Beyond this monument to childhood two real horses fidgeted, harnessed to a hearse across the street. Every so often one of them shook its colossal head with a clatter of harness, or shifted its weight, putting down a hoof the size of a clanging breadboard. On the box the driver, in top hat and gold earring, was trying in vain to get someone on his phone. He looked impatient as hell.

The sight of Adam amazed her. Miranda couldn't remember when he'd looked so handsome as now, standing in front of a bank of hothouse flowers with Julie beside him. For some reason people were lining up to shake hands with them, almost as if the wedding had already happened. Julie herself bloomed amid the general warmth of flattery. Her colouring was pale but warm; forget about blood thrusting its way round the dermal layers and think instead of spring foliage struck through by sunlight.

'Darling!' Adam further astonished Miranda by offering a semi-stranger's air-kiss; then directed a shaft of beaming hospitality at each of her friends, shaking hands – 'Hello! Hello! Hello!' – before swerving to greet someone standing behind them.

That left Miranda and Julie swapping introductions almost as nameless strangers. Julie's smile was brilliant with unease.

Both started to say something, before Adam interrupted. 'Darling,' he told his fiancée, with happy urgency, 'there's another very old friend of mine here who can't wait to meet you…'

*

Untypically Etta was also late for the party. She'd been waiting for the chance to direct her energies down the phone at her son, whom she was committed to brandishing among this afternoon's important guests.

Unlike her public self, with Thomas she became cajoling – at times almost fluttered. She hadn't always been that way. Her uneven career had once taken precedence over everything, starting soon after she'd entered the US on a working holiday. Marriage had swiftly helped her establish herself in the media, as the telegenic wife of one Reverend 'Ministering' St Clair. Thereafter she'd given her all to the evangelical New Right and its cause of true femininity. 'Submission to her husband,' Etta wrote as editor of American Mothers for Freedom magazine, 'is the marvelous act by which a real woman becomes entitled to rule in her own home.'

Her children, primped and pomaded, had encountered her on camera as often as anywhere. Mostly the infantine Julie and Thomas were raised by a succession of immigrant maids anxious about their dodgy papers. On her spouse's show meanwhile, Etta's no-nonsense style soon transformed her into the main attraction. Seeing which, the Rev. St Clair had been much displeased, yea unto vanishing.

His desertion had left wifehood all washed up as a selling point. The children found themselves whisked away to London, where their mother's failed career at least had the advantage of being unknown. From now on it was the politics of single parenthood that looked set to showcase Etta's abilities, with the then endlessly defeated Labour party offering the best chance to start rising through the ranks and outshining her colleagues. Until Julie and Thomas had passed through the unpresentable chrysalis stage of growing up, they'd seen even less of their mother, blooming in her new identity as standard-bearer of the caring society.

So even now it was an anxious semi-stranger who wheedled Thomas to come and mingle at the party.

'For your own good, you know.'

'Yes, Ma.'

'You mustn't think I'm pressuring you.'

'No, Ma, of course I don't.' Faced with subservience even a good man may find it hard to sound patient. But Thomas managed it.

'Does that mean you will? I hate to nag. But I've told you about most of the people you'd be able to meet.'

Self-respect demanded that he couldn't give in completely. 'I might only be able to drop by. Quite late, if no one minds.'

'But you can still be there for a few minutes?'

'Of course.'

Two words that can mean anything, from earnestness through to absolute-zero disdain. Gratefully Etta noted that in her son they carried nothing but upright reassurance.

'Oh, but that'll be fine, darling!'

*

On the lawn beneath the big plane tree several guests looked familiar. Miranda knew them from other parties here, spent gabbing over champagne and jewel-like *bonnes bouches* served by waitresses who were mostly young resting actors. It took some minutes to see who was missing, but then it became obvious. Of course. Laura's friends. The realization stealthily saddened her; she hadn't appreciated how she'd taken their presence for granted. Several had seemed like family – the more so since, apart from Kitty, neither of her parents had any surviving close relations.

Many had been Laura's ex-patients who'd grown into friends. Ezra Herbert, the ancient cartoonist listed by Hitler for extermination once Britain had fallen. Maynard Wearing, in his father's Savile Row tweeds, who'd shaken off a career in international banking to work as a freelance gardener. Zak Joblonski the cult science fiction writer, in bygone years heroically poor and still dressing as if from a rubbish skip. One by one she noticed them. Their absence, rather.

There was no hint of shabbiness present or past in this afternoon's guests. Adam had always had a childlike enjoyment of meeting new people and dispensing his famous hospitality. If Laura hadn't got on with all of them, she'd never said so. Miranda recognized several just because they were famous. Hugo Petersham, a one-time lecturer in law at Oxford, had famously turned his life around to make a fortune in railway leasing. Bret Figgis, still in his thirties, had done well with themed restaurants, and was now using Uzbek money to build entire spas in outer-suburban Russia. The publicist Bryan Capstick was there too, whose most famous client was forever known for having backed over a royal corgi.

To be fair, a lot of people were putting themselves out to see this occasion in the kindest light.

'It's good to know Adam won't be on his own.'

'You must be grateful to see your father happy again.'

Some were spared embarrassment by having no idea how few weeks had passed since Laura's death. One guest, the wife of someone in the Cabinet Office, was even worse informed.

'Personally I always thought your mother used to be perfectly charming. You won't neglect to give her my regards, will you?'

But most of them were strangers. Hadn't her parents known anyone much in common? Surely it was divorce, not widowhood, that divided a couple's friends into his and hers.

Out in the Square, the hearse, for whatever reason, was still waiting. Miranda had seen Jeanette talking with the driver in his melodrama-villain's tailcoat and boots and now Richard was out there, though she was ready to bet no other guests had been unselfconscious enough to take a closer look. The driver hadn't seemed too sociable; yet Richard must have stood out there for at least half a minute, scrutinizing the wreath.

Just from how he lingered, you could see its message wasn't what you'd expect.

Eight

Etta had never dreamed she'd be delayed by anything like this. Poised for exit to the party, she'd been clicking through the approaches to New Mail, just as every other day. Her new home computer was too expensive to hum, except when starting up, like a butler clearing his throat. The paper-free desk where it stood was small and semi-invisible, in a corridor alcove handy for scanning the mail on one's way in and out of the front door.

The list of items was small and tidy; almost everything in her life, to do with home as well as work, was handled by her office staff. Today one e-mail was anonymous. 'There is a file attached to this message,' said its box. 'Do you wish to view?'

Tense and enlivened by a day full of purpose, Etta nonetheless clicked on Yes and waited.

Her determination to be off turned soon to impatience, then displeased confusion. This was something she'd seen before. 'To be followed,' read the words on the screen, inside a curlicued frame.

Last time – a few days ago, was it? – the message had stopped there. Now there came into view a further image.

Part of a broad Afghan rug. Discarded clothes and shoes; the claw feet of a mahogany bed.

'Life is for living?' read another caption. 'Maybe here, it is!!!'

Etta flushed, then paled until her mouth was grey. A mob of unwanted emotions hassled her as she moved abruptly to log off.

The soundtrack cut in before she could do so. Cheap music, to cover two voices. One male, the other female, though the quality was so bad you could only tell their sex from the garments tossed onto the floor. Etta waited while the tinny melody rambled on. What angered her most was suspecting that the film's very obscurity was meant to irritate her. And had this bloody person no idea how important things could be today?'

Above the part-completed picture, two words blinked up in heavy type.

'KEEP WATCHING'.

And then the screen went blank.

Etta's suspect list had already scrolled past her mind's eye as she reached for the off button. Certainly she knew who she did want to find on it. This might in fact be something she could use.

Even so she was rattled. Why else should she turn off her PC without closing it down in sequence?

*

Almost the last person to arrive was Josh, still invalid-pale but striding like a man leaning into his own private hurricane. As he barged up the steps and into the open front door he hailed Miranda across several other people.

'Mandy! Great party, then?'

He looked sombre and overwrought. She could see he'd come here on purpose to be riled.

'Wit and wisdom from every side, is it?' he called out. 'Loadsa tottie from division one? Best of everything an honest fucker could want?' Guests nearby stiffened and pretended he wasn't there, like Tube passengers seeing a busker approach.

He was neither doped nor drunk; that much she could see. Poor Josh was simply in that state of compressed excitement where he had no idea which emotion – mockery, calm righteousness, rage – might rush and seize him.

'Dad and Julie are in there,' was all she could say, as an appeal to whatever was left of his ingrained good manners.

At that moment Adam came into the hall.

Miranda couldn't believe it.

'My dear chap,' he exclaimed to Josh, as if to someone significant from the world of work. 'How are you? You *are* looking well!'

Nine

Getting into the flat unnoticed had been nothing, there were so many people around. The rest of the house was being done up yet again while the owners were in France at their place near Grasse. Cast-iron Edwardian fireplaces were giving way to historically correct surrounds in Georgian marble and in the broad hallway a newish hardwood floor was being replaced with flagstones. On any day here several different trades were at work. With so much traffic in and out, some days on every floor, the place was permanently open, right up to where alterations were planned for the roof garden. The whole site, begging for it. The two intruders had been ready with a story about timber preservation, but in the event no one gave them a glance.

At the end of forty-five minutes, when they still hadn't found what one of them said they'd wanted, cushions were put back and plumped and a couple of opened books replaced face down without losing the page. If they hadn't been successful, no one could say they weren't thorough.

'Messy buggers, aren't they?' said the younger man, after they'd moved a heavy sofa away from its place. You could see the shape of the big fucker's footprint in the dust. 'Anyone'd think they had it in for us.'

'Some people have no consideration.'

If they had left evidence of a break-in neither was known to the authorities. And in case they were challenged they'd agreed in advance which one would do the talking, just so they looked like they always worked together.

Twenty minutes more yielded nothing. While one of them made a last check behind a shelf-load of books, the other breathed on an oval gilt mirror and wrote in the condensed vapour with a gloved finger, 'Fuck this'. Expressionless, his companion, as the one in charge, took a handkerchief and rubbed the glass clean.

At length the younger man said, 'Buggered if we can't take something. Don't want the day a total bust.' Though not particularly short he was strutty, in the way of a born sidekick.

Hunkered down, the other was concentrating on replacing the books in their original order. He looked up, red-faced from crouching. When you needed a hand on a job like this, he guessed some could be all right, and some could lose their bottle any number of ways. And then there was this one. Who might still turn out to be a barking mad cunt. Not that you'd care to say it.

'Just don't make it show.'

'Aw, sod it. Nothing here you'd want to carry, anyway.'

No mess, then. No grief neither, for a while.

*

It was too early to leave the party, so Miranda sneaked off to her old room. In the tilting chair by her desk she swivelled absently through a full circuit, wondering how long she could stay up there in peace. The room was a record of her life right up to when she'd left home: a shrine to innocence.

Treated with love indoors and with care by everyone they knew, she and Josh had grown up scarcely aware that, close by, the glow of other households' prosperity was blinking on or off as casually as the lights on a fruit machine. Among one or two people in the Square itself, iffy deeds were rumoured – serious time served, indeed. But only on account of unseen victims losing money electronically, in a seeming mirage of big-time villainy. Ordinary crimes, banal and disastrous, with sluicing body fluids and small returns, happened in some other world.

Living in the Square, with its quiet houses full of good things, anyone from beyond had seemed like dream people. Traffic noise was vague, even though audible at every hour, sure as the moon's pull. Lying awake sometimes in a midsummer dawn, watching the pattern of her hand-blocked wallpaper fade up, Miranda used to imagine she heard the whole city vibrate. Not from night flights and distant trains, but in response to the hopes and apprehensions of its newest arrivals. Every few heartbeats, so she pictured it, there came another disembarked soul, cherishing a cardboard suitcase and not speaking enough English.

How few such people must have felt like her old, protected self as night faded, waiting to break into the next few hours of her own wonderful life?

*

But Josh's old room was now bare. Hearing him move about, Miranda found him pulling out empty drawers and wrenching cupboards open, to find only decorators' materials. His precocious mural of their parents was gone; and it took a moment to realize what had happened. The walls were papered over with pixies, in readiness for Josh's bedroom to become a nursery.

'It can't just have disappeared! Mandy – someone must know where it is. Even if it's all in bits.'

He meant a mobile sculpture, finished just a few months back. Josh had taken as inspiration his biology classroom's standard replica of the human body, with inner organs in coloured plastic that fitted together like a three-dimensional jigsaw. Using parts from just such a model, he'd made an intricately balanced helix, incorporating some finery from every landmark ceremony from baptism onwards. Breathe hard on it, or give a gentle shove, and heart and bowels would dance a minuet with such emblems. In the world beyond school Josh was already winning prizes. But nothing had made him so proud as this.

'It can't have gone,' he repeated, futility being a first response of the helpless. 'It took me six months to do that. And Mandy, what's happened to all our photos? There isn't anything that's not missing!'

True, the wall of photos under glass with all its scenes of infant good cheer, making sandcastles or picnicking, was also gone. It was impossible to ignore how much of their home was newly unfamiliar. Amid a dull surge of dismay Miranda saw how much of their childhood must have been banished, scrunched up in darkness at the back of some storage space or thrown away.

Josh himself was too choked up to speak. His blotched face wore a look of fierce abstraction from trying not to weep. Oh, please, Miranda thought – please don't let him shed tears where people might see! Not even from rage. However much of an idiot poor Joshie can be, he doesn't deserve that.

Breathy with effort, he said, 'I only came here to get my stuff. So where is it?'

Seeking explanations Miranda found Etta, in the kitchen supervising the caterers. But instead of answering any question, Etta proved determined only to come right back with a demand of her own.

'Does anyone know what the matter is with your brother? I'm sorry to have to tell you this, but one really can't pretend he's looking at all happy to have been invited.'

'How can he have been invited, when this is his home?'

Etta's expression didn't change, though one could swear a rush of adrenalin deepened the colour of her eyes.

In fact Josh now boarded at school even in the holidays – as Etta missed not a breath in pointing out. 'So I think you'll have to agree: it's by Joshua's own choice that he no longer lives here.'

*

'So who *have* I got to see?' The hearse driver had had it, but badly. Close to, all creped up but without the dignity of his horses and grand vehicle, he looked like an actor sent to the wrong location. Cornered in the hallway Adam was mystified.

'I wouldn't mind,' the man said, 'if only I'd been given a job spec that didn't bloody waste my time.'

Josh sauntered up, haggard but self-possessed. To the driver he said, 'What he needs now,' indicating his father, 'is to see the wreath.'

All around them people were falling silent. Striving not to bluster, Adam muttered, 'Sure,' adding as an afterthought, 'If you would.'

The undertaker went out to his hearse, not the least bit appeased. What was a wreath like this one supposed to mean, anyway? Sure, it was all done properly, with white carnations and everything. But what about the words on it, once you took a proper look? Someone was definitely playing silly buggers, and at his expense. As he carried the wreath back he made a point of not hurrying.

On his way Josh passed him, leaving at a fast walk. The lad was hunched around himself, to hide the fact that now he really was in tears.

Etta's rage, on seeing the wreath and its message, was something special even though she remained almost wordless. 'At a time of celebration like this,' was her only comment, in a quiet steady voice.

Driving home, most people told each other much the same. Really no one should have found it necessary to dwell like that on Adam's previous marriage. Let alone suggest the details of how the first wife met her end.

You Said She's Where?

Etta was swift to take responsibility for whisking the wreath away and binning the thing. But first, carrying it into the scullery, she blunted the kitchen scissors quite badly in her haste to cut away each wired bloom making up the inscription. Not even in the compacted darkness of an Essex landfill was this message to survive.

What it no longer said once she'd done was: Rest In Pieces.

Ten

Miranda didn't go back to the flat. Instead she drove at speed twenty miles out of town, to keep an appointment with Laura.

St Aldhelm's stood in one of those freakish patches of country quiet that survive in several places round the edge of London. There wasn't even a village; the little medieval church had been built for a congregation of shepherds and their families, living scattered across a semi-wilderness of downland. Impossible nowadays to stand at the top of its square flinty tower and not be accosted by the sight of Canada Wharf grouped with other toybox towers down on the plain. But from the churchyard below, all you saw were woods and fields and an approaching avenue of beeches mis-shaped by upland weather.

Miranda's mother had been baptised and married here, from a house in a scabby pre-war suburb just behind the horizon. On days when the wind blew from the direction of London, the empty pastures filled with chimes from ice-cream vans cruising a nearby housing estate. But no matter how fragile and menaced, this still appealed as the first countryside Miranda could remember. Even now its homely mysteries of steep woods and pillowy fields gave her a childish pang of wonder. It was partly because of this that she'd decided here was where Laura should be buried.

She trudged up the path to the churchyard, still in her basic-black party dress with dinky matching bag. Her arms were goose-fleshed by the early-summer breeze. In the Mini she'd changed her patent Gucci pumps for some clumpy trainers that made her look like a skinny child dressing up in adult clothes. From the car's boot she'd taken out a florist's bouquet of Madonna lilies. They'd been there all through the party, not nearly cool enough, and were starting to wilt.

Near the wall at the top of the churchyard lay a half-dozen newish graves, mostly with too-shiny headstones including the pair commemorating her grandparents. As an economy in keeping the place up, a clergy stretched almost to invisibility had sectioned off the recent memorials with an electric fence and rented the rest as grazing for a flock of Southdown ewes. On the neglected gravel path, all sheep droppings and bird's-foot trefoil, Miranda paused and crammed the florist's wrapping into her impractical party-going bag, then went to place the flowers above where Laura's head would be.

Longer than grief. Wherever she'd first heard the words, they revolved in her head like a tune that wouldn't go away. Yet the world went on as if nothing was wrong. She noted, as if standing just out of register with the rest of herself, a disbelief at so much normality. The wind tugged at her hair and clothes and soughed in the beeches; a murmuration of starlings banked overhead; and three miles up an airliner passed inaudibly as if moving with the invisible stars. In the lane the racket of a motorbike vanquished every other sound, and on a neighbouring hillside a tractor and baler crawled to and fro, full of tidy purpose.

The selfishness of grieving amazed her now that it was her turn. God knows, she'd wondered often enough at the hospital how it must feel. Like this, then, while everything else in life became a movie you might as well not watch.

The bike had turned off the lane. Under the avenue's wavering sunlight and shade it was bucketing up the track to the church. Miranda got ready to leave, unwilling to hear the place noise-polluted, much less see another human. Most likely it was someone paid to come out here and keep the place up. The bike cut out behind the church and peace returned, filled by the random bleating of sheep. She expected an odd-job man to appear round the south porch, or maybe an old rocker in a clerical dog-collar.

But no. She had a moment of non-recognition, seeing just a teenager shambling like one of the dispossessed. Only then did she recognize her brother. Josh had brought flowers too, incongruous festive blooms, mostly red tulips. He carried them with their heads pointing down, in that arm's-length fashion with which a man might pass a woman her handbag, as if not physically connected to it.

He stopped on the other side of the grave and half-placed, half-dropped the flowers onto it without acknowledging her. For a moment it seemed they'd meet and part in unbroken silence.

'Joshie...' She couldn't help speaking pleadingly. He looked up at her without a change of expression.

'Why didn't you say you were coming here? You know I'd have given you a lift.'

As if that would've mattered to him. 'Why didn't *you* say anything? About coming out here?' His anger showed no chance of pity, for himself or anyone else. 'Since it's Mum's birthday.'

Whether or not Miranda was his only ally in the world he glowered as if straight through her. 'Is it because you're ashamed, too?'

No need to ask what he meant. 'Look!' Violently he indicated the grave. Uneven turf squares lay with their edges still raw; meanwhile a growth of plantain and docks was also establishing itself. 'Look at it! They haven't even got round to putting up a headstone.'

'I'll get it done, Joshie. I mean, I'm sure Dad's got all that in hand. But I'll see it's done soon.'

Josh ignored her. The breeze ripped at his open leather jacket. 'What can be done?' he said, as if to himself. 'What can anyone do about all this?' She knew he didn't just mean the slovenly rectangle of grass at their feet.

He turned a dull steady look on her that made Miranda's heart contract in pity. 'Ought you to bother? Hadn't you better leave all this, just as it is?'

'Why? What do you mean?'

'Are you sure you want to be caught showing them up?'

'It wouldn't be showing anyone up – just ordering a gravestone.' Though she couldn't help fidgeting under his stare.

'You know what I mean. Go on, say it. How long *will* it take you to get your degree? It's years before you won't need Dad's money.'

'But – you know how generous Dad's always been. He's Dad, for God's sake. How could he possibly let us down?' Just mentioning such a thing – if only to deny it – made her feel shamed.

'*You* know what it'll cost you to qualify. How much time. And money. How hard you'll have to go at it. And you'll never be officially poor enough for a grant.'

She couldn't tell if he meant to accuse her or sympathize. Maybe Josh himself didn't know.

Anxious or not for herself, on Josh's account she did feel a tug of fearfulness. All the way here she'd failed to shake off the thought of his bungled histrionics at the party. The hearse. That undertaker, who'd had every right to be furious.

'Was that you just now, back at the house? Coming up with that wreath?'

He stared obstinately at the ground. Not even offering a denial.

'Was it you that hired the hearse? Josh – for God's sake! Your're the one who mustn't go making enemies.'

'You see! You don't trust them either.'

'Don't be stupid. I wouldn't dream of making a pointless attack on them – on Dad and, um, Julie. What business is it of ours?'

He mumbled, 'It makes no difference anyway. If they want us to quarrel with them, so they can feel good about themselves – *yes*, Mandy – yes, they do! – if they're hoping for a fight, what difference does it make what either of us says or does?'

'But why? Why scrap with anyone? Just because we feel … maybe left out. It would be so …' She sought a less self-important word than dishonourable, and settled for 'piddling'. 'Anyway, it would be futile to pick a fight. To act like a total loser.'

The appeal to his pride went for nothing.

'You're so keen to be nice. And reasonable.' Josh drew out the last word, like a defiant old lady mouthing an unfamiliar obscenity. 'Where's the justice in that?' He hesitated – turned away – then back again – stiff and purposeless, weathervane-style. Abruptly he said, 'You staying or going?'

'Joshie…'

'What?' It came out like an accusation.

'In the long term … What you say about Dad funding us… I mean, I'm sure—'

'Don't be. Just you wait.'

Eleven

'Are you eating or what?' Jeanette stood in the kitchen doorway looking purposeful and holding four glass flutes.

'I suppose so, thanks.' Miranda slumped in the Windsor chair at the head of the big pine table, still in her sneakers and party black. Thank God there'd been no one in the car to see or hear her, on the way back from the churchyard. She'd turned up the radio so loud, its noise could almost have liquified your inner organs.

At least she'd been inaudible while shouting at other road-users. That was one of the things she'd never done before. The other was driving dangerously, which had got her back in record time.

She hadn't known herself.

'God, I'm knackered – Oh, Christ, it's my turn to cook!'

'Don't worry about that. We're getting in a curry. It's on us.' Jeanette glanced aside and lowered her voice. 'We did think you mightn't be up to it.' She'd been there when Miranda had bought the lilies for Laura's grave.

'"We"?' Surely Richard and Alicia were too frenziedly bed-bound even to notice if the world still turned.

'Sure. The champers too. I know we were bingeing on the stuff earlier, but this is from us to you.'

Such sympathy was bound to catch her short. *What is this! Jesus. Don't cry, woman ...*

It was Alicia who unwittingly came to her rescue. Strolling in from Jeanette's room, to judge from what she wore. Seeing her in Jeanette's black roll-neck cashmere and designer jeans, for once Miranda was grateful at the prospect of strife. There was more to pay at this address than a steep rent: Alicia was forever borrowing without permission. Jeanette, size ten and therefore at risk, was frankly unembarrassed about keeping her wardrobe locked most of the time. Miranda was just thankful that most of her own clothes were too large to be filched.

Unflustered, Jeanette glanced at Alicia then at Richard following her in. All the while putting out glasses, she said, 'I'm planning to wear those later.'

Alicia slid into her seat. Looking good, what else? Turning to Richard she said of her purloined clothes, 'They are rather super, aren't they?' She stretched her arms above her head and smiled up at him with a flashbulb brightness that made the poor guy respond in kind before he knew what he did. Only then did Alicia's behaviour make him redden with embarrassment.

Not one to nag, Jeanette said as if changing the subject, 'Champagne?' But shook the bottle hard before she opened it.

The explosion lost several glasses' worth. Behind Alicia, whose blonde hair instantly darkened and dripped in tatters, the wall ran with fizz.

Somehow Alicia stayed a graven image of indifference as she got up to change. But even she couldn't surpass Jeanette's rendering of, 'God, how clumsy! I feel such an idiot.' Not for nothing had Jeanette's prospects filled her teachers at RADA with expectation. She might not have the looks for an insecure life of stardom. But once established as a character actor, at a hundred years old she might still be in work.

Richard was all confusion. It was impossible not to feel for him.

'Sorry about the fizz,' Jeanette said to the room in general. And hurried out to buy some more from the place at end of the street.

'Please don't worry about it,' he called.

'I'm gone already,' she trilled, and shut the door behind her.

The usual flat-share wars.

Miranda filled Richard's glass then her own with what was left. The two of them sipped in silence, he no doubt promising himself that Alicia's character might yet change. Meanwhile Miranda heard her own bedroom door being opened. Scarcely stopping to mop herself dry, Alicia must have gone straight off to pinch something of hers.

And what, in there, had she knocked onto the floor?

Alicia's scream wasn't exactly that, though it ricocheted off every surface. It was more a battle cry, signifying anger rather than dismay.

'Tell us what it is, then,' Miranda called out. She heaved herself out of the chair and followed Richard into the bedroom.

Alicia was rigid with outrage. 'Ugh! Urgh! *Urgh!*' Deeply offended, or what? Though somehow one knew that even her shrieks would be ladylike.

The only thing to be seen on the carpet seemed to be a frivolous dressing-table object, something Adam had once bought Miranda in a junk shop for storing rings and other jewellery. One of those upright stands covered with green baize, in the shape of a hand.

'So what's the problem?'

Alicia looked at Miranda as if she didn't believe anyone could say so heartless and low.

Richard picked up the fallen object and turned it end over end, taking care not to dislodge any of the rings threaded onto it. Whatever this was it wore a wrinkled glove. He gave a bark of laughter – mostly from surprise. 'Look at this!' he said, proffering it wrist end first. 'Whose idea do you think this was?'

'Oh… I *see.*' Miranda laughed too, but likewise from shock. Even facing something far worse than this, professional pride, if you want to call it that, would have made them compete to show their total cool. 'It *is* a severed hand. A real one, I mean.' After a pause she tried saying, 'Not very original, is it?'

'*We've* done better.'

'Oh yes! The leg!'

Last year's rag week had been a turning point for relations between Faculty and students, after several people in balaclavas, mostly from Richard's year, had emptied a carriage on the Tube by passing an amputated limb down its length. Fierce words had been uttered by the

Student Disciplinary Committee with all parties wearing academic dress for the occasion. Not surprisingly the rules for ragging had been changed forever.

'It'll never be the real thing, now,' Richard had said. Two years ahead of Miranda, he was well liked as the class clown, to the pratfall born. Outside the Dean's office though, at first all he could do was blush and look sobered. 'After this we might as well be hired entertainers in a theme park.'

Miranda peeled the glove up and looked more closely at the hand. 'It could have been worse. I mean, in worse condition. And it does seem to have come from a dissecting room. Look, you can still smell the formalin.'

Even as she spoke, she twinged with guilt – just a bit – at making Alicia stand still for this parody of self-possession. Given the chance it was a game they all played at St Ted's.

'Bit dried out though,' said Richard, noting the parchmented skin. 'Can't have been watered for several days.'

Alicia had recovered enough to feel excluded. 'You're both sick!' she managed. And stalked off with an hauteur that would have redeemed any exit line. Richard hurried after her.

Miranda stood turning the hand over and back. With no witnesses to make her fake unconcern, another thought was growing and settling in her mind like the first dull symptom of some fearful disease.

So why here?

Twelve

'I suppose everyone feels an idiot,' Miranda said, 'at a time like this.'

For the moment no one answered her. They were waiting unconsciously for the distant sound of the big front door being closed behind the two departing police. When it came, everyone stirred as if normal life had been resumed. They were sitting round the debris of supper, with Jeanette dispensing a fortifying round of Irish coffee.

'I'm not sorry I got you to make that call. If that's what you mean.' For once Richard's take on the world wasn't fogged over by lust. As though the evening's distractions had left him looking if not older then for the first time more man than boy.

Miranda said, 'What I do mean is, it's stupid of me to think sending for the police has somehow exorcised whoever left that thing.' She didn't care to admit it, but the yellowed hand, with the knobby carpels protruding from its severed pemmican wrist, was an object of horror. If it represented an attentive unknown malice.

'Just as well that whoever it was must've committed

a break-in,' Jeanette pointed out. 'Nobody feels paranoid when they report one of those.'

'Yes, at least the police took that seriously,' said Alicia, whose manner had recovered to become quite crisp. You couldn't help wondering what gritty memsahibs, totally proofed under fire, might have flourished up her family tree. 'I thought that woman's attitude wasn't bad, actually.'

Two uniformed police had been round almost immediately. The man had made an effort to be reassuring – he'd even confused Richard by apologizing for nearly going through a door ahead of him. The woman, pretty, low-voiced, with a look of stroppiness tamped down, had done most of the questioning.

But their queries had stopped short at why this big house, its rich pickings untouched, had been illegally entered. As to the theft of body parts ... well, ensuring security in any big London hospital was so daunting, it might as well be an impossible quest in a Greek myth. Only last month in a lift at St Ted's Miranda had overheard someone senior in crime prevention bitching about the sheer variety of theft she met with. Watches, pillowcases, sheets, bedpans, soap, surgical gloves, calculators, a crate of floor polish, a canteen microwave. Frozen chicken wings. Beefburgers...

'I know I shouldn't really be freaked.' Miranda upended the last of the Bailey's into her coffee. 'But I don't think those coppers were telling us to forget it, were they? I mean, it's not as if they looked bored or pissed off. Do you think?'

Such things can happen any time, they'd said. Report

anything else if you feel you have to. But usually it doesn't mean a thing.

*

All the same. She'd half expected it when the next thing came to pass. Why else hesitate before picking up whatever it was off the floor?

It must have fallen out of the glove. The writing was dense and tiny, as if this were a document designed to look cute in a dolls' house.

At the top, the flat's address, followed by:

Look closely. Because this is just your Prologue.

Thirteen

Coming home one evening that month, Etta almost ran up the broad front steps. Not in haste but on a charge of energy got from a day of victories. She exchanged a brisk acknowledgment with the stony-faced porter and pressed a button for the lift with an upbeat abruptness seen in most people only when drunk.

And the day so far *had* been good. Against her more wary hopes, three of several meticulously planned campaigns had just delivered. Since leaving for work eleven hours ago she'd had herself confirmed as chairman of a housing association, and director of a regional youth orchestra as well as of a newish but growing cash-for-questions lobbying company. Now it was time to change out of her Aquascutum emerald suit with cobalt trim and into zircons and tailored black silk, for a reception being given at the Guildhall for the Prime Minister.

In weeks – no more – Etta's prospects had expanded well beyond expectation. If she wasn't yet riding to victory on an escalator, no longer was she hauling herself up a ladder with missing rungs. Next month she'd be moving house. It was hard to believe that the current address, in a service block on a skyline near Crouch End, had once been such a relief after the early months in London, spent in those two and a half rooms in Walthamstow. On returning to England, Etta had had to work in a call centre, first selling then hiring and firing. She and Julie had shared the double bed – plastic button-backed headboard with gilt trim – in its too-small room while Thomas slept on the sofa.

Now this place too could be wiped from Etta's account of herself. Since Julie's collections of glass animals and stuffed toys had been removed, there was nothing to show who lived here anyway. Sure, much the same anonymous deep-pile interior would greet her in Maida Vale: everything chosen by a firm of decorators, with engulfing sofas in pale mushroom brocade and reproduction watercolours of racehorses or Spanish dancers. Banished though would be the picture-window panorama of central and south London, so displeasingly littered with tower blocks. In its place would be a delightful prospect of the Grand Union Canal, where houseboats and the barges let for partying waltzed between white Victorian villas, under a tunnel of plane trees. In what passed for private in Etta's life, at last the word suburban was free to take root and bloom as a term of happy censure.

Haste notwithstanding, on going back out she still checked the PC for incoming mail.

Unlike this morning she was forearmed. Habitual self-possession usually meant that even alone she behaved as if for an audience. Nothing was allowed to make Etta look surprised a second time around – even now when dread nudged her as much as potential anger.

Just as well. Again there were the rose and midnight blue intricacies of that Afghan rug. On it lay the tossed clothing. The man's hand-made shoes, the woman's silvered strappy sandals. Beyond, the mahogany bed.

This time the image on the screen was expanded, incoherently at first, like an animated abstract. By degrees it became readable, as nakedness intertwined. Limbs pale as statuary seen under water, but moss-green where shadowed. This video was not the work of a professional.

No faces were visible. A canopy hid them, tied back in heavy swags. Anonymous or not, this wasn't the scene of anything sublime. Whatever they're doing no one can look primal when dubbed with music from a compilation tape. Besides, this was no long yielding fall into ecstasy. Tricksy sex ruled here, valued for its ingenuity.

Were the voices superimposed, as well as the music? In the little that was uttered there were breathy dips and hitches that suggested not. But against a track from The Best of Ravi Shankar neither of the people on the bed sounded identifiable.

The music stopped just as the woman's voice, taut with concentration, said, 'Oh… all right…'

*

In the home office at the Albany Square house the eye didn't know where to rest. No department-store window, properly designed, would care to show this many goodies at once. Or so Etta confided to her daughter, *sotto voce*, trying to give Julie a proper sense of her own good fortune.

You Said She's Where?

Two days before the wedding the assembled presents were piled six feet high in a drift of professional wrappings and glitter ribbon. There was no call to provide the bridal couple with anything even slightly needful; no bath towels or steam irons here. Instead several offerings combined frivolity with physical size and weight: a gentleman's mahogany valeting stand, five feet tall, on which to lay out next day's clothes and toiletries; a baize-lined box from Harrods containing a croquet set ...

By the time the presents were due to be displayed at the reception venue one of them had begun, very faintly, to smell. While it was in an overflow pile in the big kitchen/family room any untoward whiff had been masked by cooking smells. On the first day this was no match for mackerel in gooseberry sauce; it was also eclipsed by next morning's kedgeree. The parcel in question was skilfully wrapped in thick embossed paper you could almost refashion as a party frock.

It was duly transferred to the reception's fabled setting at the Inns of Court, in the medieval hall where in 1594 A Midsummer Night's Dream had had its first performance. Here the strongest odour was the dizzying scent of lilies. Between chiffony swathes of baby's breath, they were arranged with white lilac and Golden Fantastic roses on two dozen pedestals leading to a matching arbour, a cave of flowers. As the team of caterers started to unpack, the whiff from the invisible contents of the box had all sorts of competition. A long buffet table nearby supported a landscape of food: oysters heaped on a moraine of broken ice; mousseline of lobster in shining aspic like a Winter

Queen's castle; pâté de phaisan en croute resembling a rustic folly under its pastry leaves; pretty garden plots patchworked together in the form of charlottes de légumes. There was terrine de bouillabaisse, saumon en coquille, turbot remoulade, aiguillettes de canard sauvage, ballotine of chicken and jellied ham bourguignonne, truffled fois gras galantine rolled up like a sumptuous fabric sample, and a big sea bass whose reproachful eye was actually half an ounce of caviar. A carnival parade of fruits and puddings culminated in a four-tier wedding cake of raspberries, cream and white chocolate, apparently supported only by repeal of the law of gravity.

But the small, smart, energetic firm of wedding contractors responsible for displaying the presents eventually had their suspicions. A game of hunt the smell – by now hardly floral and not at all cooked – was on, amid ribald and tasteless guesses as to what they were looking for.

Luckily the young woman who opened the box was a moonlighting trainee chef whose specialities included offal. So, no squeak of dismay from her on looking inside. Something made her exclaim though, mainly from curiosity. As her co-workers gathered round, the general response was laughter, some of it nervous. Mostly they were bewildered.

Best to put it aside until its true significance could be checked with the bride's mother, as the occasion's organizing genius. It was she who'd taken personal delivery of it, from another family member.

For some hours it stood on the floor in a lobby, against

a faint background melody of wedding bells, followed by the nearer tuning of a string quartet, then the swelling sound of well-shod feet and glad voices.

*

Josh hadn't been there in the church. And his phone was off. Unsure whether to be worried or relieved, at the reception Miranda sought in vain to find out where he was.

Adam and Julie were inaccessible of course. Everybody looked greedy for one minute of them. Julie was peerless in a trailing white silk Empire dress. Somehow it warmed her pearly colouring, the kind so prized by eighteenth-century classical painters. Adam was both dignified and as flushed with excitement as a boy of sixteen.

But Julie's mother, all wide-brimmed hat and busyness, seemed momentarily free. Lying in wait, indeed.

'There's something you need to be shown,' she told Miranda, and led the way out of the main hall. Aflame with self-control.

In the lobby Miranda found herself confronted across an opened so-called present, hatbox-shaped. Nestling in several pretty colours of tissue paper was a garlanded bridal veil, handsomely made, with fake orange-blossom flowers in white silk. It framed a stylized lacquered mask in the likeness of a not-quite-human pig, presumably inspired by – what? Totem art of the Nootka or Chinook? A Shang dynasty ogre? A spiralled Maori tattoo?

Not quite Josh's work. But close?

Whatever the original quality of craftsmanship and design the overall effect was foul. The garland cradling the mask had become badly soiled, by a brown stain centred on two gory hearts excavated from the carcass of a large mammal. Presumably a pig by way of sustaining the porker motif. The smell was now remarkable.

In handsome italic print a thick deckle-edged card read: 'Act I. Hearts and Smarts.'

After a moment's puzzlement Miranda's heart fell like a switchback ride derailed. The hatbox stood inside an anonymous brown cardboard box identical to the one she'd been handed by the porter in Reception at the hospital. Worse, she recognized the label, addressed via her to her father and stepmother at the wedding venue. It had been she herself who'd placed the box in Etta's hands.

Groping for her best consulting-room manner she said, 'I'd bin that, if I were you. Before it becomes a serious health hazard.'

No way would Etta dream of discarding such an offering. Not before it could serve as prosecution evidence.

'Don't you feel the shame of the person who could send this?' She fixed Miranda with a bayonet stare. 'I know I do.'

Outside, almost drowning her precise enunciation, the musicians were playing a salute to the history of the grand, ancient building, with an arrangement of Mendelsohn's Overture to A Midsummer Night's Dream. The brouhaha of the reception was still growing, a wall of sound in celebration of the good wishes being poured out here as if by all the world.

Except for whoever had troubled to contrive this surreal and repulsive thing. In vain Miranda sought a reply that combined tact with self-respect.

Etta said, 'One thing you have to understand: both you and Joshua. This' – indicating the putrefying artwork at their feet – 'has got to stop.'

Miranda felt an epicentre of anger shift inside her. It left her almost too surprised to speak. 'Surely,' she bluffed, 'the best way to find who sent this to me would be to put it on display. Right now, in front of as many people as possible.'

Without a word Etta retreated.

Fourteen

Another party, in another time.

Josh was high on hope back then; impatient to see what eighteen would bring. He wanted to feel the same forever, since it seemed impossible that he could relish being alive any more than this. Not his *life, just life itself.*

He didn't much care to join the party. His father might grumble at his absence, even while his mother, calm and easy, might say it was still a chore for him to mingle with their middle-aged friends.

Downstairs the house reverberated with voices; a sound as steady as a well-tuned engine, punctuated with laughter. He was alone in his room, exploring the newfound land of his latest video equipment. Over the last two days its ramifying discoveries had nailed him there night and day amid polystyrene packaging ignored where it had fallen.

Best of all, it counted as class-work – a fact he'd made much of when anyone came to his door with talk of feeding or sleep. Right now across town at Putney in an Edwardian mansion flat by the tidal banks of the Thames his friend Ollie Gunton had been told to lurk steadfastly by his own PC, ready for transmission. He'd been informed that if he didn't report perfect reception his only prospect was perdition.

The video was Josh's latest in a series of techno-Annunciations. It had been planned as part of a split-screen composition he'd devised for A-Level, and showed the Square's back gardens in a time-lapsed film, their trees burnished by early-spring light or shoving their branches about beneath a chill wind. People also featured, like mute actors crossing the stage in a prologue: a couple of tree surgeons, semi-acrobatic in the topmost branches of an aspen; an unseasonal lunchtime drink on the York stone patio, courtesy of climate change. And now this party's overspill into the garden, where Josh, attempting a theme of impermanence, had figures fade up, disport themselves and ghost back into nothingness. He was at a stage of life when such sporting with notions of mortality turned him on, innocently intrigued, like a tourist at the scene of some ancient massacre.

One camera had been installed at the top of the house, angled down from the window of the box room where the sewing machine lived and laundry got sorted. A moment's concern occurred to him for this carefully contrived arrangement, featuring for support a stool balanced on top of a small table. Shortly before, he'd heard footsteps that were meant to be inaudible, as of two or three children engaged in hide and seek.

During the party the room should have been put out of bounds. Loping up the stairs, ready to surprise whoever they were, Josh recalled the adage that a quiet, unnoticed child usually meant mischief. Somebody was certainly close at hand; he could hear tiny creaks and percussions, no louder than a couple of mice rustling about in a roof.

Shit, there was someone in the laundry room; he could hear them through the half-open door. If they were kids mucking about, he could see them before they guessed he was there. A full-length mirror, leaning outside the room to help check the fit of sewing alterations, would show their legs and feet. Lengthening his stride, Josh reached the last turn of the stairs. The one about to consign him to his life's next chapter.

As he climbed, somehow he'd already felt his heart begin to thrash like an injured frog.

Of course they weren't about to see his reflection.

Not while they were standing there fucking.

At first he'd failed to take in even that much. Momentarily the heart and brain reject what the eye sees all too clearly.

An act of violence outside of time. He didn't need to see their faces to recognize them: neither her unfocused look of triumphant yielding – head lapsed backwards, tongue wet and lolling in her open mouth, eyes almost turned up into her skull – nor how his father had Julie's wrists against the wall at head height, battering himself against her, hard and deliberate, as though trying to nail her flat. He had clenched his whole self against the onrush of the end.

Josh's first pang drowned him in unreasoning shame, at knowing and understanding more than he saw. This was no innocent act of lust, a quickie sufficient unto itself. Unheard, as well as unseen, he retreated, numb as if from some gross injury that would later bring obliterating pain. Soon he would feel rage; till then he fled, as if from himself.

Some hope.

*

Stalking off through the other wedding guests, Etta left Miranda looking at the fouled veil, full of fears for her bloody stupid brother.

Poor sod. All his life, loved by everyone. And now acting rash and hopeless, in danger of being crushed beyond recognition by the weight of his own hostility. Thank God he wasn't here. A malevolent spirit, that's how he'd be seen, out to blast the happiness of hero and heroine at the start of their story together.

And now time for the speeches. The best man was Henry, a friend from Adam's time at Balliol, nowadays awesomely successful as a divorce lawyer. Everyone warmed to his tact, when he began right away by hinting that Adam's life 'had indeed been overshadowed by loss'. 'All the more reason,' he said, 'for my old and cherished friend and the multitude of well-wishers here present to be grateful for the life-restoring presence of Julie, his bride. Without the happiness and sorrow of his former years, the couple's present joy could not be valued as it truly deserves.'

By the time Henry finished speaking, Adam seemed to have grown in dignity, and Julie's beauty was transfigured far beyond mere prettiness. Even two of the reception's over-qualified waitresses had tears in their eyes. Several people there sighed with relief at Laura being so gracefully remembered, and Miranda softened into gratitude at hearing her father so described as a good man.

Adam's speech was more spontaneous – no trace here of the inflexible self-assurance he showed in public life.

As he stepped forward he looked almost vulnerable and everyone was ready to love him for it.

The room already brimmed with goodwill as he began his thanks 'to all of you who have helped to bring my wife and me to this time and place'. Almost none of his audience wore the bright vacant look that can afflict even sensible people when listening to speeches. With every word the noise of general approval deepened and grew. Starting as a faint groundswell of good cheer, like a smile shared by all the room, it rose to laughter as Adam spoke of 'today's rendezvous with destiny'. And good-natured heckling broke out when he declared his gratitude 'at being surrounded by such troops of friends, who must surely be evidence of a life well spent'.

'So which of you will believe me when I say that I'd expected to go through today a disappointed man?' The noise from the guests fell; their shared smile broadened into anticipation.

'Let none of you mistake me. What I'd anticipated wasn't dismay,' pausing amid laughter. 'It wasn't reluctance,' raising his voice above the growing response from his audience. 'It wasn't even, dare I say, one single nano-second of reflection. But why – why' – struggling now to make himself heard – 'am I telling you this? When the one thing hasn't happened that I thought would make this day less than complete? When, after all, what my wife and I both dreamed of has come to pass?'

As the room fell nearly silent Miranda found herself wishing she wasn't there. That, like Josh, she just hadn't been arsed to show up.

You Said She's Where?

'When my wife – my wonderful, perfect wife – my wife has confirmed what we've wanted to hear all along – that I'm to be a family man at last!'

The general roar of approval lasted nearly a minute.

*

So he doesn't prize her after all. Not any more. He's too dishonest with himself to know it, but she's his ex-daughter now.

All the more reason to show him what family values really are. She might still do.

That first time in her flat. First time in every way. Just so I knew I could do it. The hand was just something extra.

And now. The beauty of it is that she'd find something out as well as him. She needs to know her place, now he can't be counted on to look out for her. It's only doing her a kindness in the end. She's got no business acting like he still cares.

Real life's not like that.

Fifteen

They were always undignified, the last few paces to the world's edge. Then you thrust the ground away from under you and morphed from battery hen to condor. Plus, an instant before the moment of triumph, the sensation of a balloon inflating in your chest at the same old thought: what if I've just imagined the safety checks?

The Beacon's grassy prehistoric fort was the perfect place: one kick, and earth and sky opened around you like sailing into a picture. Right away Miranda felt the sweat cool on her face and neck. All that thermal gear felt so stupid on a warm day – until a few seconds after takeoff. The silence overlaid everything except the rustle and pop of the giant canopy inflating. At her back the others' voices were a separate soundtrack fading down.

Up here you were one unmoving point; it was the world that slid around at your command. Today the North Downs, an azure fantasy of themselves, lay along the limit of sight. She flexed a wrist to tighten one of the risers. The horizon tilted, made a long smooth motion sideways and up, and was shouldered aside by the steep profile of Upping Combe. Now, in mid-afternoon, one side of its woods was already cut off from the sun. Fifty yards below her a bright russet speck hovered over the shaded treetops: the top view of a kestrel, sunlit and motionless, sharing the same updraft. Swept by the canopy's shadow the bird flapped away confused.

Behind and below, the others circled, suspended in a skyful of drifting primary colours. After several minutes of not being earthbound the spirit still went on unclenching. It came on by degrees, that relief at pushing the world away from you. Sometimes you could be floating about for ages, watching one skyline rise up behind another, before the thought occurred: I'm here – I'm free – I'm *here*!

She did a circuit over the village. The farmhouse and its ragged little orchard looked subtly wrong from here, like most scenes of early memories viewed from a new angle. A dirty Volkswagen Beetle stood beside the black-clapboard barn that used to be Kitty's studio: Jeanette, down late from another unmissable job opportunity in town. Though the silence up here shocked you every time, on summer afternoons the countryside below was more crowded than you'd think. In the great park of a National Trust house a mile or so north, a horse show was in progress: two arenas and a village of marquees, with several acres churned up by ranks of horse boxes and four-wheel drives. On Cottingdean Common, immediately below, a small herd of motorbikes scrambled inaudibly round a sandy landscape of birch trees and gorse. Three hot-air balloons seemed not to move, lined up in the sky half a county away above the High Weald.

As always on a clear day with a breeze from beyond the

downs, in the distance at least a dozen other paragliders were airborne. Often groups that big could show up the best thermals from miles away, rising together as dense as seagulls over a fishing boat. For a single flier, even a tractor and baler could give off enough heat for a steep instant ascent. At random Miranda made the scarp revolve beneath her, centring on where their cars were among those parked along the edge of the summit. Not everyone below in their party was recognizable, even unhelmeted. Frances, who liked to come along but didn't care for all that dangerous unpredictable flying, sat straight-shouldered in a folding chair, reading a book. Rob, a useful-looking guy and the one who'd got them all to train in the first place, was laying out his canopy. Meticulous and impatient, he was preparing to try that day's final quest for the perfect lift. Most people, when barging towards a drop like that, went po-faced with the effort of looking unworried. But when Rob jumped, you could see he was focused to a point that left anxiety itself blanked out.

Even at this height he was identifiable, from a bandaged foot. He'd been carrying out a perfect landing last week on rough pasture, feet together, knees bent ready for a parachute roll if needed. What he hadn't noticed was the stub of a broken sapling, Sabatier-sharp, which had gone right through the sole of his boot.

A mishap like that wouldn't have stopped Miranda coming back either.

Her phone rang. Zipped into a pocket of her flying suit, it was almost inaudible; instead she felt it pulsing, like an external bodily organ. So she could fly straight while checking out the call, she changed course. The canopy's shadow passed over the cars, then swooped away, faster than an unopened parachute, as she floated three hundred feet above the Beacon's north slope.

She had to angle the phone carefully to stop the sunlight blanking out any text. It read, 'HiYaMirnda! UWthTBigRd&YeloShUte Wot!NoHndsAsULokAtThs? WotIfUGoIn2AFullStall? BcosIStlWanUIn1Piece!'.

*

It was a relief down in the pub to be hearing about someone else's grief. Anything to ignore what she'd done next.

'I wouldn't mind so much,' Jeanette was saying, 'if the great man hadn't lied to himself as well as me. He'd looked so pleased at how generous he was being, when he asked me along.'

She'd been on tiptoe with anticipation, after an A-list movie director – only schlock-horror, sure, but famous or what? – had followed an introduction at a first night by inviting her to celebrate his fiftieth birthday. And no – this wasn't dinner à deux nor anything like, even if he did ask her to wear a corset and high-heeled ankle boots. When the agency's van delivered it, Jeanette's full costume had turned out to be the best Victoriana that money could rent: velvet bustle, frilly parasol, silk gloves. Nothing synthetic, not even the achingly heavy hairpiece.

'Everyone must let me take this much trouble for them,' he'd told her. 'So that we can all fit in with our wonderful venue.' It was to be a lunch party in a famous mansion, all pinnacles and indoor fountains, built next to Hampstead Heath for a successful High Victorian painter whose speciality had been soft porn on a theme of classical antiquity.

'It was obvious something was up when his PA showed me through the dining room. I could see it was set up for hundreds more people – literally – than you could find costumes for. And then there was this freezing back room with a dozen people in it who looked just like me, only half of them were men. Getting changed. I mean, once we'd sized each other up, you could see we weren't actually going to be guests.

'One girl walked out right away, leaving a terrible atmosphere. But I thought, hell, it's bound to be interesting. The food and drink should be amazing, and you can't be in the same room with that many people and not mingle somehow...'

...How could she? For God's sake, how could she have dropped the fucking phone? Miranda was even angrier with herself than with the damned poxy anonymous caller. *And from up there, probably in full view of him.*

Face it, why make the call, if she couldn't be watched while taking it?

Somehow things were made worse by the distance it had fallen. As if, when it burst apart in some stand of bracken, there'd have been any difference in it hurtling down from just fifty feet instead of hundreds ...

'...And the guest list was stupendous, once you saw who'd started turning up – Ta...' Jeanette gulped down a dreg of Bass and handed her glass to Jack, who was splitting a round with Thomas. On the way to the bar and back they each had to stoop beneath the pub's ancient gouged rafters.

'…Only, it turned out that they didn't give us a single sodding sandwich. The PA woman was in a panic once the first guests came in and we hadn't been shown our positions. I mean, out in the garden – I can't believe I can bear to tell you all this – pretending to talk to each other. In sodding tableaux, to go with the period setting. *That's* what he'd meant by fitting in. At least if you medics want to get started in life all you have to do is work your balls off.'

'Can't be worse than being a writer,' said Rob. He was shortish and strong, a bull-terrier among the rest of mankind. But progress on a so far uncommissioned novel had left him more self-absorbed than if he was pregnant for the first time. Miranda and her friends had met him as one of the weekly helps at Albany Square. During the day he had a smart starter job with Adam's publisher as a junior editor. It was the publishing director who'd recommended him as their cleaner, in compensation for his facetiously small salary. Inevitably he was known as Rob the Swab.

He said, 'The market wants us young. If I haven't made it by thirty-five, the best publicity I'd get would be if I did the murder of the year.'

Jeanette turned to take her beer. 'Cheers, Jack.' She carefully slurped the meniscus bulging on its surface and said, 'At least I don't have to worry about a clock running.' Physically she was what she called 'a scrappy little git'. But she could amaze by changing in almost any direction once she stepped out on stage. 'If I was a gorgeous total stonker they'd never let me near the character parts and by forty I'd be stuffed.'

Frances, who seemed to live to utter mild good-humoured irony, said, 'Tell me how you'd play a pathologist and I'll copy you at all my interviews.'

Everyone laughed except Richard, who'd spent the day in silence, looking like an invalid. Alicia had cried off at the last minute, giving no reason. It was costing him to have left her behind; but he'd already promised to be one of the drivers.

'As far as I'm concerned,' Thomas said, 'I've arrived already. Compared to what I used to expect.'

Thomas couldn't have helped being a late starter. Without money or contacts to give him a hand up, right into his twenties he'd been directionless. Several years had sneaked by with all his energies gone for nothing. As a gopher: in security; in debt collection; at a car dealership.

If he'd thought about medicine, all it would have meant to him was the surgery on the mean street in Walthamstow near where he and his family had lodged. The local practice worked out of a tiny house in a Victorian terrace, whose front garden consisted of a glinting mosaic pavement two paces deep.

The merest coincidence had brought him to St Edmund's.

'What turned me round for good was when I worked as an underling at an auction house. Cynical buggers, stringing you along with phoney promises of getting promoted. Then one day I was at a house sale of contents in Hampstead. The guy who'd owned the place had been a heart surgeon. The day he retired he'd set about drinking himself to death – efficiently, like you'd expect.

'And that's what did it for me. I thought, you jammy sod. Fancy having a job so great, you'd rather die than go without it.'

There was a momentary silence. Then Jack said, 'I've got a superstitious reason for my career deadline.'

The others waited. He said, 'Great-great-uncle Reg.'

'I'll ask,' offered Jeanette.

'Great-great-uncle Reggie was twenty-seven when he copped it at Mons.' It was partly as family, so Jack said, that he'd been hired to help restore the murals on the main staircase at St Edmund's. The artist himself had spent his last leave there, getting a name for himself with a composition of modern-dress figures, angular but solidly rendered, on a theme of healing.

'So if I haven't started making it by then, I'll be well pissed.'

*

10 January 1946
Stumblehurst Farm

And now it's daybreak. The sky an unsullied whole, the dim land stirring. I picture the earth arched over by an infinity of souls. Not the dead, but we survivors who lost everything we loved. I suppose I'll have to go and pick up more kindling today before it gets soaked through. The wireless did say rain.

It's something, I suppose, that I make myself do these chores. Get the rucksack – army surplus, like so much here: scratchy blankets, knobbly towels – will the damn war stay with us forever, even in small things? Get the bike. Let's hope there's no one else in Upping Combe, picking up sticks. Expecting me to say good morning.

Grief is supposed to numb you. A lie: all these months I've been a skin filled with knives…

Miranda shut the diary – guiltily, even though she'd been given a free hand with everything left in the farmhouse. Kitty's handwriting, of course. She'd probably long since forgotten it existed.

All this stuff. How could Kitty bear to part with so much? But then, how could she have lived amidst this landslide of debris? Almost every room had degenerated into an attic; no wonder there'd been almost nowhere Miranda and the others could unroll their sleeping bags. Impacted papers exploded outwards every time you opened another drawer, and the dust could have been rolled up like felt. The sitting room curtains could only be closed by draping their hem over hundreds of books stacked on the floor. And a big metal clothes rack on casters, the kind you got in shops, nearly blocked the top of the stairs. It was untidily covered with a sunlight-stained bedspread in frilled yellow satin, beneath which God only knew what past fashions hung forgotten.

Some things may have been quite valuable. The brick floor of Kitty's incongruously neat studio was stacked with numberless works: canvases, painted boards, sketchbooks the size of a church bible, all carefully inclined together according to some system. Jack, as ever, had prowled the house and barn in a state of half-concealed agitation; impossible to say if curiosity pricked him on as a fellow artist or a would-be looter. Either way, he'd been within a breath of offering to sacrifice his morning's paragliding so he could help.

If you hadn't known, you'd never guess from the prevailing squalor that this was how Kitty had always lived. And now, where to draw the line between trampling her privacy and finding out keepsakes that would call up her image in years to come? What should be left for Josh to choose from? If the remaining furniture was to stay behind for tenants, Miranda was duty bound to empty every drawer and cupboard. She shut the diary back in a trunk under the bedstead and resolved to start with the worst of it all. Maybe the walk-in larder, with the big forgotten jars of home-bottled fruit. On the labels, written in brown faded ink, the dates had been scarcely believable.

Outside, framed by a deep-set bedroom window, the Beacon reared up against a perfect sky into which every so often one of the others would float. Miranda turned from the view and tried again to set to.

Sixteen

'Hello, Wendy? ... Hi—'

'Who's speaking, please?'

'Wendy – it's—' Something made Miranda wary enough to pause. 'Could I speak to Adam, please.' She realized she hadn't spoken so formally to Wendy since she was ten years old, on the day Wendy had started as Dad's secretary.

She was calling from a busy landing, on the way to take that morning's blood samples in place of an overstretched house officer. It was on a big stone staircase in the old part of St Edmund's, designed by a Victorian architect better known for building country houses with complicated service areas. The place echoed from other people's haste, and she found herself compensating for the noise by almost shouting.

'Uh, hold the line please—' Wendy sounded faintly embarrassed. As if she'd like to gossip as usual, but dared not. 'I'll just see if he's there.'

After waiting a while, Miranda sensed her morning start to dim. The daily unreasoning joy of just stepping out into the street, the mild brilliance of early summer, even her own tactless good health compared to the look of various outpatients from Urology getting into the clanking old lift nearby – all suddenly faded. Wendy had never before claimed not to know Adam's whereabouts.

Plus there was the unexplained piece of paper in her pocket.

Put both facts together – Wendy's reluctance to talk freely, with this latest, unbelievable bank statement – and she could guess what many patients went through when facing the primary symptoms of a feared and degrading illness. All it took to deaden every other feeling was that first feather-touch of doubt.

Was there really no mistake? How could so many hundreds of her allowance have been cancelled?

Adam was in a meeting, said Wendy, when eventually she came back on the line. No, he wasn't sure when he'd be free.

Later too Miranda called in vain: from the lunchtime line-up in the canteen, then while emerging from the loo after the day's one long-deferred pee. She tried again in the evening bus queue, and on the ride home standing up in the gangway. In the end Wendy actually sounded curt. What made it worse was that she clearly disliked whatever she'd been told to do. She'd never been so unprofessional as when she finally said, 'I don't see why you can't just call him at home.'

It was Etta who picked up the phone in the Albany Square house. She always seemed to be there now, doing whatever people did as grandmothers-to-be.

'Is it important?'

'I want – I need – to talk to Adam.' Miranda's own lofty tone surprised her.

'…No, I don't know when he'll be in… Perhaps you could be more precise about – Ah… I'll see that you're contacted … When? Why, surely on an issue like this you can expect a response as soon as possible.'

*

In the event the call came next Saturday morning from Etta. '…I'm afraid today's the day that Adam has to go to Frankfurt.' She added, 'Of course you're welcome to discuss things if you wish.' Miranda hesitated, uncertain what the woman meant. In a tone of brisk concession Etta said, 'I'll tell you what: instead of hanging about here I'm sure you'd much rather come out and be treated. Would the Garden Room suit you?'

It made sense all the same to call by in Albany Square, and pick up some more books.

But Miranda's door-key wouldn't work. For some reason the locks had been changed, and she had to ring the bell. To be answered by Julie, with an audible 'Oh' of surprise. She looked flustered, as if one of them wasn't supposed to be there.

Miranda had never seen her stepmother outside a formal occasion. It took some moments to realize that this becomingly rumpled figure was Julie's usual self: pony-tailed hair in a state of designer dishevelment, and feet prettily bare rather than just unshod. The embodiment of leisured pregnancy.

'Right… oh, right, yeah.' Julie nodded, at pains to show she understood as Miranda explained why she was there. But she still didn't move from the doorway.

'I'll just come in then,' Miranda said, by now feeling like a salesman on the coldest call of his life, 'and find the things I need.'

'Yeah, right. Why don't you come in here,' indicating the television room, 'and make yourself at home?' Julie's anxiety was almost as if she'd been caught in adulterous mid-tryst. 'I'll just get Mum to help. I'm sure she'll know where your books are.'

'No, that's all right—'

'Oh, but you can't find them without her! I mean – they've been moved—'

'I'm sure Dad would know where they are. Is he here?'

Poor Julie had had it with being out of her depth. 'I'll just get Mum,' she muttered, and bolted.

Miranda gave it ten seconds while she examined her new situation within her old home, then left the room. The house was full of domestic noises, the loudest from a vacuum cleaner wielded in a neighbouring room by Rob the Swab.

On the first turn in the stairs Etta accosted her, with, 'We can't have you wasting your time here. Why don't we help you, by sending on whatever it is you want?'

A phone rang in Adam's home office. At the same moment Adam himself hurried out of the main bedroom with a coat over his arm. He was carrying his laptop and pigskin briefcase.

'Darling!' He hesitated, passing Miranda on the stairs,

with a gesture of I'd love to kiss you, but – see! – I'm burdened. 'How are you, lovey? I'm sorry I can't stop – but that'll be my driver calling.' He looked both animated and uneasy. Pointlessly he added, as he swerved into his office, 'I'll get it!'

Etta scurried after him. There was a murmured exchange between them, in which Miranda overheard him say, 'It's not me in particular she wants? Not a social visit? I mean, it is just about money?'

Etta's voice, also intermittently audible: '…Oh, that won't be at all necessary…'

He was still saying goodbye to Julie behind a closed door when Etta and Miranda each drove away from the house. They were headed towards Hackney's most happening brasserie, where Sachertorte and Apfelkuchen were served with a choice of coffees from six different time zones.

'Now,' Etta said, once they were sitting face to face in a window overlooking the great trees and dog-fouled sward of Victoria Park, 'I need to know exactly what it is that's troubling you.' Her concern looked unavoidable as death itself.

Once more Miranda outlined the unsuspected bad news delivered by her bank statement.

'Have you no grant?'

'Not while my father's earning as much as he does.'

Etta's features sharpened into a question mark. 'Are you sure of that? In any case, why can't any of your mother's relatives help you pay your way?'

'All my grandparents are dead. That leaves my great

aunt Kitty, who's got no idea how far her money will have to stretch.'

'But do you consider that you need the extra money?'

'What extra money?'

'The extra money you say you want in addition to the sum handed out to you by Adam.'

Miranda's blink rate shot up. She took a precautionary deep breath. 'I'm not asking for an increase. I wanted to know why my money's been cut.'

'Are you trying to say that you feel you don't have enough to live on? If so, it's something we should consider very closely indeed.'

Through Laura's job, then working at the hospital, Miranda was bound to know something of how their poorest neighbours got by. 'Often we're hardly doctoring people's bodies at all,' her mother used to say. 'Just suppressing the symptoms of other things.' How easily money worries could show themselves as chronic poor health. Toast and Marmite substituting every day for a boiled egg. Bus fares saved by walking home tired from work.

It seemed a lot less now like news from a distant country. She could easily have got by with a share of her mother's savings. But apart from books, clothes and not much jewellery, everything Laura owned had been left to Adam.

She said as much; then Etta, implacably attentive, replied, 'You do know your father's counting on you? As the sensible one in the family. He's been through a difficult time and it's up to all of us to show consideration. Not least where financial matters are concerned.'

Miranda ignored the implied reference to her brother, as a career idiot. 'It'll be easier – in a way – to make do with less if I know that later on there'll be enough for Josh.' At least this year of his schooling had been direct debited in advance.

'What are you suggesting? That your brother's due will be withheld from him?'

'No. But I'm still glad to hear it.' She couldn't help noting the other woman's actually quite becoming flush of combat. Etta, she'd just bet, took no stimulants except coffee and kept her use of alcohol to pursed sips of champagne at public toasts. This was a woman who lived her life as one adrenaloid high, on willpower alone.

'Of course your father assumes that Joshua will want to take a gap year, like his friends.'

Miranda was gobsmacked. 'No! – no, that's not what's planned. Josh can't wait to go on to art college. And the school says he's almost guaranteed a place at the Slade.'

'Well, if that's what he thinks will happen, perhaps you'd better be the one to tell him otherwise – that it could be very difficult for other people if he went to college right away. It really would be best if he doesn't take the money for granted next year.'

'What about the following year? How will that be different?'

'He mustn't be impatient, that's all. I'm sure most people would be only too grateful for a year in which they can find themselves.'

'Actually Josh was doing rather well at finding himself.'

Etta stayed silent. Wielding discretion like a blunt weapon.

'He's already been spotted as exceptional. Besides, how'd he be supposed to pass the time after his final term?'

Etta's stare didn't waver. 'Now, Adam has thought about this very carefully. And he does have Joshua's education – and his need for independence – very much to heart. Which is why among other things he's prepared to allow your brother a chance of access to a particularly useful job with good prospects of on-site training—'

'Training for what—? What can he possibly do that would substitute?'

Etta hedged. 'Your brother won't just be a student, you know. He'll have opportunities for work experience too.' Seeing Miranda's expression she added, 'Some of us, you know, have been very glad of what we've got from the university of life… I'll be frank with you. Now, this is what's proposed…'

After a bit of window-dressing, the facts emerged. Josh was being offered 'a position' in a bakery owned by one of Etta's town hall contacts. Maybe later he'd be allowed to do clerical work, 'on one of the firm's excellent computers'.

Merely hearing her found Miranda doused in shame. Part of her took in every syllable of 'chance to practise self-reliance' and 'in on the ground floor' even as she pictured Josh's own initial bewilderment.

When Etta was done, Miranda managed to say, 'I'd still like to talk to Dad. To ask him if Josh can't have something different from this. Perhaps if some of my allowance…'

'If you don't think you need so much of Adam's money, I'm sure he'd have a good use for it.'

'What I meant—' Speak slowly. Breathe carefully. 'There's no point in me going short. Unless it helps Josh.'

'We'll see. There's only so much now to spend on you both.'

For precaution's sake, Miranda said the obvious. 'If I had less money than Dad proposes, I'd have to go out and work quite long hours. As well as studying. It would make completing my degree really hard.'

Etta deposited her napkin on the table and signalled for the bill. 'Naturally the choice is yours. Adam's spent a lot of money on you so far. But if, say, you decide after all this time that you've changed your mind, and don't want to do medicine, just tell us.'

Seventeen

The cork shot up like a firework, then fell four floors to the street below. Within the next week everyone was leaving the flat-share; so they were marking their departure with an impromptu party beside the roof garden's fishpond. One morning, coming up here, Miranda had surprised a heron in mid-swoop. A fat goldfish was striving in its claws, and its wingspan was like a near-miss from a jumbo. Rather prematurely, the pond was now covered by a dense metal grid, part of the changes that had also given the smart little back garden a new lawn and a swing even though their landlords' longed-for baby wasn't due for a month.

They'd always known that if Alicia's cousin downstairs did get pregnant their part of the house would be given over to nannies and a playroom. Alicia had left already, to live in borrowed lodgings with her boss from the Bedford Square literary agency where she worked. They were waiting till they could move out of town, into a beautiful neo-Doric rectory in Gloucestershire. She'd always seemed an entirely urban creature; recently though when someone said as much she'd replied, 'There are serious people near Bamford Peverel.' She probably meant royalty.

Alicia didn't say how Gerald had afforded such a house 'on top of everything else'. Meaning of course his fiercely contested and never to be mentioned divorce.

Throughout the brisk transfer of her affections Richard had been unexpectedly dignified apart from having wept at least once, audibly in the bathroom. He too was gone, preferring a sleeping bag on someone's floor to remaining at the scene of his casting off. In any case he too might be leaving London, being one interview away from a place at Princeton doing research in forensic psychiatry. At any other time the news of his likely place there would have filled him with unselfconscious happiness. But it came on the worst day of all, with Alicia unbendingly calm and Richard himself looking murderous. Miranda and Jeanette had sidled out and eaten in the pub that evening and no one had dared say anything, even to congratulate him.

But tonight by chance it was Jeanette who was being feted. If only in the short term her career was sling-shotting her further from home than anyone. She'd got her heart's current desire, as a gofer helping to take Shakespeare on a tour of the Pacific rim. With the National, no less. It was going to be an ordeal of long-haul flights, and endless PR for all the cast. Drudgery like that didn't fall much short of the young Chaplin having to paint scenery and sweep floors between takes. But Jeanette couldn't wait.

It was one of the year's perfect evenings, bright and benign, with middle-distance landmarks – Canary Wharf, the still-half-clad Gherkin – looking over the rooftops as clear as paintings on glass. Out on the pavements of Upper Street, restaurant tables were crowded with white trousers and bare arms, and people looked easy, as if expanded into a happier sense of themselves.

So too Miranda's friends. They'd just helped carry her sound system and an almost-final box of stuff down to the nearby flat she was due to share with Frances. Now they were lounging about, drinking plonk in their besmirched oldest clothes and suffused with mild summer warmth. She wanted to hold this moment forever, unfogged by time – perhaps one day to compare it with themselves twenty years on. Say, with Jack by then – like, please God, Josh too – at the centre of some densely networked school of art-world mavericks. Thomas, full of calm encouragement towards his patients, and swiftly promoted way beyond making up for any lost years. Rob, no longer bellyaching over his failed authorship, because life was so much sweeter as a senior publisher with large share options lending savour to anecdotes of his moonlighting years as a cleaner. Frances, lifted up above her early self-doubts, as the consultant pathologist against whom everyone else was measured. And Richard? One sure thing: he'd have risen in life far above dwelling on an old flame as transient as Alicia.

This evening had to be immortalised somehow. Miranda went to get the splendid Leica that Adam had given her last Christmas.

On the way back she glanced down from the landing window. Dusk was filling the streets with shadow while up here the late sun was almost blinding. The mews behind their house looked smaller from above, like an architect's model. You could tell whereabouts in it the new flat was, from Frances' terracotta window boxes full of flourishing dwarf marguerites, planted to match her white net curtains in finest Swiss cotton.

Was that a movement inside? Back upstairs she asked Frances who it could be. Crossing the rooftop garden to look again, she saw a man come out.

'Actually he's not moving like an intruder,' she said as Frances came over to join her. Moving at his ease, he climbed into a yellow Lotus parked nearby which roared to life with a show of potency.

Right enough, she'd missed the obvious truth.

'Oh, Phil's my stepfather. He said he'd swing by with some of my stuff from home.'

Of course. For God's sake. He'd even been pocketing the door keys as he walked away.

'Was my stepfather, I mean.' Frances' mother had recently sued for divorce, having left for California and an actor chasing local fame on the fringes of TV. Miranda thought the breakup sounded rougher and dirtier than Frances had implied.

'How far back did their marriage go?' The first rule of any medical training worth a damn: never fail to ask a half-invited question.

'Fifteen years. Slightly more.' Not long after she was widowed. So Phil was the only father Frances was likely to remember. A copper, hadn't she said? CID?

'My vanishing parent seems to be taking most of the family assets with her.' Frances spoke lightly, true to her ironical, mild-mannered self. 'Not least the benefit of her company.'

Any benefit to herself, was what she meant. What right had anyone to say some people don't still need a mother at twenty-two?

She added, 'Maybe in California she'll get what she wants. She's been so confident about her new man – about his prospects. He's only taken one suitcase, she said. Travelling light, as if he was rich already.' She hesitated, then added, 'Poor Mother. She was always discontented, working where she did. Even though it was quite grand.' A theatrical agency somewhere in Mayfair.

'I think she hated being labelled just a secretary or whatever. She was always critical of herself, as well as going on at me. Obsessing over being presentable enough – I mean, in that musty, nineteen-fifties sense. How I hated it, when she tried to invite people to dinner because their house or job impressed her. Most of them never dreamed of inviting her and Phil in return.

'The worst rows were over money. She was forever nagging Phil to overextend himself and move us further up the hill. Verdayne Grove. Ladyhill Park Drive. I used to picture some of those names engraved on her vital organs.'

Miranda knew to answer lightly. 'At least she's not leaving you in a pit of poverty. Living down there.' The mews had been built to serve the same terrace they were about to leave. Once this little street had been a place of hardship. Its outside walls would have been shaggy with soot like an unswept chimney; indoors, there'd be no hiding place from the smell of manure. A dunghill tang must have touched every handkerchief and rank uncased pillow.

But now its cottagey façades were newly painted in a range of ice-cream colours. A cramped pub built for local workmen at the blind end of the mews had recently been refurbished right down to the joists. Its window-boxes held swags of begonias and busy lizzies, covering the place like a great vegetable chest wig. The plants were watered by a firm of contractors, so that every other day people drinking outside risked being dripped on.

The inside of their pretty upscaled dolls' house had proved full of light and seeming space, now that a designer had made free with some mirrored walls. Like a schoolchild seeking team points for tidiness, Frances had brought her own dimension of perfect order. On the solidly built-in shelves her books were ordered according to the Dewey decimal system: divinity first, led by St Augustine's *City of God*, and natural sciences last, following on from a handsome if foxed copy of Audubon's *Birds of America*. All with a thoroughness to be admired by any professional librarian. Her clothes – dark suits, neat cashmere, carefully pressed linen – were stored when out of season in tissue paper or zip-up bags, and entered on her PC to show what went with what. A separate computer file, saved under 'Sentimental tosh', held a long list of items from childhood: a christening robe; a dear little sweater with a nursery-rhyme motif, hand-knitted for her first term at school by a grandmother long gone. Her system of logging useful phone numbers – its back-up, copying, printing, storing and cross-referencing – was a thing of wonder. Gratefully, Miranda had even pinched it for her own laptop right down to some of the passwords.

'That's not plagiarism,' Frances had said, half-serious. 'You're just using the obvious system.'

But for someone who kept mementoes from every part of her life, she'd let none of this hoarding instinct show. No tottering dusty heaps of folders or loose paper here. The flat shone with care and smelled of furniture polish and flowering plants.

'We're lucky to afford that place.' Gazing down into the shadowy mews Miranda tried not to make it sound like a question. But from things Frances had said, she wondered. Did she too risk being stalked by debt?

Frances' gaze slid away over the neighbouring rooftops. She wasn't always one for confidences; sometimes you might as well try to shimmy on a glacier. 'Oh, Phil says his mate just sees us as someone to keep the place aired … It's not bad, is it? Especially compared with this whole street when new.' She had a good eye for social medicine, whether focused on leukaemia clusters or likely causes of the Black Death. '…Is everything of yours packed up?'

'Yup. I can't believe I needed all that stuff.'

'You ought to keep it; you'd be surprised at what you can re-use. Or sell.'

It had taken nearly a week to convert books, tapes and armloads of clothes from so many metres of space into boxed-up kilos. Nothing extraordinary about that. It surprised her though how little was worth trading once she'd sold the car. Say, for next week's rent. For groceries, even.

The pages of her life were turning faster than expected. Still, she'd hardly be slumming. Just letting go of one or two daft luxuries.

Eighteen

In the room where students and staff gave blood, this week it was Mozart. The recording was left over from last term, when a couple of doctoral students in clinical psychology had been experimenting with music to see if it reduced raised pulse rates and breathlessness among first-time donors. Argument still grumbled on among the nurses about whose taste in composers was medically the soundest. It was agreed that the only real disaster had been when someone tried to introduce whale songs. Those didn't last the first morning.

But as Miranda was leaving late that afternoon, suddenly the overture from The Magic Flute was clashing with the fragment by Pachelbel that her phone travestied every time it rang.

'Hello, Mandy. I was afraid I wouldn't get you. How are you, lovey?'

'Dad!' The voice of his old, reassuring self was like an echo from a lost age.

'Darling … could you possibly call in here – home – on your way back? We really would be very grateful.'

'Dad – is everything okay?'

'Fine – just fine – if only you and I could talk together.'

'I can be there in an hour.' Two tubes and a bus. Without a car, she was re-learning the city.

'Take a cab and I'll reimburse you... No, really – I'm sure there's nothing seriously amiss...'

Sure, nothing seemed wrong as she let herself in – it was Rob, of all people, who'd offered her a replacement key while muttering something about keeping Etta in the dark. Her father even stood up and greeted her with an embrace, just like he used to.

The place seemed ready for yet another party. Glimpsed through the open door to the drawing room a long table bore a banquet of finger foods. At its centre stood a birthday cake the width of a spare wheel, with tropical-coloured icing. A party for Julie, going by the not-so-dense candles. This summer whenever Miranda happened to be here there'd often been some kind of junket, with food and drink for shoals of people. She couldn't believe it only seemed that way, from coincidence. Unseen by her could the rest of their time really be taken up with, say, frugal evenings of cocoa, Scrabble and companionable silence?

Adam, usually scrupulous in standing aside for women, this time led the way into his study as if it were a pub that might turn out rough. Immediately Miranda caught a whiff of something that shouldn't have been there. No wonder the window was open as far up as it would go. After a couple of heartbeats she realized what it reminded her of. The horrible bridal artwork sent to the wedding reception.

'I had to put it in here,' Adam said, 'so that it wouldn't

upset anyone else.' He pointed towards his desk. 'Once you've had a proper look, I can throw it away.'

What you don't want to see, at first you misinterpret. Kitty had once described how, going home one day in France during the war she'd stopped, to wonder why such odd-looking washing had been hung out from her neighbours' balcony. But there'd been no mystery, nor even any laundry. For a second or so she just hadn't wanted to perceive that the local military police had hanged a couple of resisters, from their own house front.

At first sight the line-up of objects on the desk looked harmless: just part of a series of pretty Russian dolls. They must have been bought in a set, then re-painted. As with the anonymous porker-and-orange-blossom confection sent to the wedding party, the standard of work was good. You could easily see who each figure was supposed to be. The larger one, wearing a familiar baggy leather jacket, was Adam. The smaller, almost as pretty as in real life, was Julie.

Although the hollowed-out Julie likeness could have held at least another statuette, it was empty. Except for a turd.

Not artwork of course: the real thing. In a public gallery perhaps it wouldn't be a surprise; just another exhibit, shown with a caption confirming that the DNA it featured was the artist's own.

But here. A typewritten card bore the words, 'At the Heart of You'.

'Julie's asleep upstairs. This is all rather a shock, in her condition.' It was the first time Adam had said anything directly to Miranda about the fact that she and Josh had an unborn sibling. He looked more exhausted than enraged: a man with good intentions cruelly betrayed.

Miranda could scarcely bear to answer. As if not speaking Josh's name would mean this message wasn't his after all.

She said, 'Let me get rid of this.' The sooner the better. As if it had never existed.

After it had all been flushed or binned, she went back to the study.

Adam said, 'I know you must feel the same about this as I do. Who wouldn't feel concern for someone in this much pain?'

'Oh, Dad... what now?'

'I'm glad you asked that. You must agree that your brother needs help. And you and he have always been close.'

'Tell me what I can do.' She didn't stop to think whether she meant, for Adam, for Josh, or for all of them as fragments of their once treasured family.

'I knew we could count on you. He can always see someone at the school – there's a counsellor they recommend. Alternatively there's this very good man we know.'

'A consultant psychiatrist?' Miranda's voice rose half an octave in disbelief. 'Dad? Can't you just imagine what Josh would say to that?'

'Yes, but... Mandy, darling...'

Like many gifted speechmakers Adam could also use silence to impose his point of view. Having paused for emphasis he said, 'From the rest of us it would seem like interference. You know how proud Josh is. But if you could help, I'm sure he'd consider you an ally. As the family peacemaker.'

Dismayed to hear herself, she blurted, 'I'll talk to him. Maybe I can see him on Saturday.'

'A promise is a promise,' as she and Josh used to chant as children, 'and we must keep it.' She felt as if jumping down a chute whose bottom was in darkness. But how could they – she – do nothing?

'Darling Mandy. In the end, I know your brother will be grateful to you.'

Nineteen

The nurse pulled open the heavy fire door that led from the old cloisters. Josh's school came in three styles: the medieval bit, looking both beat up and cherished, where anniversaries were celebrated and the headmaster entertained likely benefactors; the Victorian quad, full of massive Gothic fakery; and the modern wings, where most classes took place. They were headed for the office of the Health Education Coordinator, down a nineteenth-century corridor of stone mullions and garish stained glass.

'Of course sensitively pitched issues of all kinds are an important dimension of Dr Ferguson's work here.' The nurse, who'd introduced herself as Mrs Ansty, was dressed more like a politician than a health worker, in a cerise jacket and skirt, a high-necked white blouse, and 'good', if punishing, high heels. Her manicure was perfect, with nail varnish that matched the suit. She whiffed of reflected aspiration: an inflexible good servant.

Miranda had talked Adam out of deploying the very good man, with his Harley Street consulting suite rented by the hour like a bordello. Someone from the school might at least know Josh personally.

Outside the counsellor's office Mrs Ansty paused and confided, 'Dr Ferguson is very concerned that we can be able to facilitate appropriate support for Joshua. Of course we always operate outside any constraining framework of a morally prescriptive kind. Ah – er – Joshua… there you are.'

Today, his old open-faced self. Thank God.

He too seemed puzzled about what was supposed to happen. His 'Hello, Mandy' came out as a question, half bewildered, half hopeful.

Before Miranda could say anything Mrs Ansty announced, in her discreet funeral-home voice, 'I know Dr Ferguson will see you now, Joshua,' and conjured him out of sight.

Miranda sat and waited. Would Josh be in there for the whole hour of a formal psychiatric session?

After a while the usual school-day noises became more noticeable. A music class several rooms away was rehearsing a song, over and over, by someone who might have been Brecht. She became aware of how many lone figures moved about on various errands during classes. If they were staff they politely didn't look at her; each pupil briefly stared. At one point Mrs Ansty reappeared in the distance, then vanished; Dr Ferguson's room must have two exits. Miranda got up and pretended to make a serious study of several glass cabinets holding trophies for things like chess and survival in the wild.

Why had she meddled? She could hardly believe how obliging poor Joshie had been about this interview. As though he actually wanted some parent-substitute to show concern by interfering.

She was just re-reading the captions to some – actually very good – photos taken on a school trip to Petra, when the office door opened again and a man she took to be Dr Ferguson motioned her inside.

There was no sign of Josh. Dr Ferguson quickly closed a further door and gestured at her to sit down. He was dressed young for someone of her parents' generation, with a shaven head that suited him better than most and nearly hid the fact that he'd gone grey.

He drew up his chair and looked at her across a neo-Victorian leather-topped desk that seemed nearly as big as a billiard table. No intimate chats here, sharing the edge of one another's breath and sitting knee to knee. He looked defensive and out of temper: had her brother just turned around, from the old Josh she'd glimpsed outside back into his new angry self?

Silence. Miranda looked at Ferguson; he eyeballed her back. She counted while twenty-eight seconds ticked away on the wall clock behind him. If he meant this as a professional ploy, it had nothing to do with his particular training. According to the school website, he'd got his doctorate (Gonville and Caius, Cantab.) in a branch of biological sciences.

In the end she did what he probably wanted and said something at random. Had Josh, she asked, said anything about the various anonymous 'messages'?

Ferguson held her look. 'What are your thoughts on these incidents?'

'What I think about them should be obvious and doesn't matter anyway. The thing I want to know is what's going on in Josh's mind.' God help her, she'd been a total coward, last time she'd talked to her brother. What she'd actually said was that if he cooperated, and turned up here today, her own allowance might not be cut. Now the thought of it made her squirm.

'Joshua does show considerable resistance to the truth, in several ways. Let's start with what happened on the occasions in question.'

Miranda waited. Then gave up and demanded, 'What about them?'

'I refer to the items sent by Joshua with what must be seen as evil intent. Yet he absolutely resists confronting his responsibility for either of these.'

This she couldn't believe. Her brother? The most straightforward being she knew, this side of honesty as a pathological condition?

For a moment she was speechless, looking at the only two explanations for what Ferguson had just said. One, that Josh was lying. Two, that he'd been slandered. The first was impossible; the second, not to be borne. Josh could be an idiot, but she'd trust him with more than just her life.

But if he hadn't sent the two vile ceramic artworks, then who had?

'I'm sorry,' she said. 'But I really think this meeting might be, um, premature. Look, I am – truly I am – terribly sorry – if you've been misinformed. I mean, if you've been led to take certain explanations for granted …'

He seemed not to hear. 'I really am inclined to recommend to you, and to Joshua's father, that some more appropriate course of action should be adopted.'

'Such as?'

'I would strongly recommend a stay in the Abbeygate. It might do a great deal to help him find his sense of perspective.'

The local nuthouse for millionaires. Miranda wanted to head-butt the wall in self-punishment. She stood up.

'Where did he go?'

'I don't think we can profit from this interview unless you answer each of my questions as put to you.'

'He stormed out, didn't he?'

Dr Ferguson just looked at her. Which was how she knew she was right.

'You don't know Josh, do you? As in having taught him, even for part of a term?' She paused, but only long enough to know there'd be no reply.

Barging out, the last thing she heard him say, as if nothing had happened, was, 'Sit down, Mrs Faulks.'

She broke into a run down the corridor. Only several moments on did the truth occur to her. Ferguson hadn't said Mrs as a slip of the tongue, meaning Ms. He really did think she was Julie. Attending as the busy, concerned stepmother.

Ollie Gunton was in the study-bedroom he shared with Josh. Almost every area of wall was hidden by layers of pinned-up documents: newspaper articles or cartoons, bits of tomfoolery artwork by Josh, timetables for class-work, a photograph of George Bush Jnr used as a dartboard. It all looked like the flank of an armadillo whose scales weren't on straight.

Ollie was tall and pale, with that improbable dark red

hair that came over with the Vikings. In an atmosphere of end-of-term unwinding he sat crouched in front of his Mac, on whose elegant blob-shaped VDU he was stopping and starting some indifferent footage of a family barbecue. Probably not shot by him nor showing anyone he knew. Ollie was trying to start his own business tidying up other people's videos into sequences that looked meant. After getting into Sussex as he hoped, to do Media Studies and IT, he had ambitions to muscle in on commercial software design for home editing.

He appeared to expect her arrival, without looking forward to it one bit.

Was Josh there? For answer, Ollie shook his head, more like a little boy than the lankiest guy in the school.

Nor could he tell where she might find him. Only later did she note his careful ambiguity.

'But—'

'What—?'

Hard to say what unnerved him more: the look she gave him, or what he was supposed to say.

Poor Ollie. He looked as shamed as if the words were his own. But he went ahead and gave the message anyway.

*

Miranda ran towards the school's main gate, three large courtyards and endless corridors away. One master looked round a door and started to shout something, then saw she wasn't a pupil. An electric bell rang, loud enough to announce the end of the world. From doors everywhere each boy in the school broke loose. The sudden press of loud, over-energised male bodies lasted fifty yards. By the time she reached the main gateway, the place had emptied just as promptly. In the wide tree-hung cul-de-sac outside, the only thing that moved was a shabby black-and-white cat slinking across the road. With a bird-noise equivalent of breaking glass two blackbirds clattered out of a shrubbery nearby, fighting each other in mid-air.

Standing outside the gates she fell to futile obscenities. Poor Josh. She'd wanted to behave sensibly, on everyone's behalf, and she'd ended up supping from a short spoon with morons like Ferguson. Miranda wanted to sob aloud, to kick the nearby wall and bloody it with her fists. So much for the great growing-up project, enabling her exemplary career as the woman she wanted to be. She reached the noise and movement of the local High Street, hearing nothing but Josh's parting message.

He hadn't said where he was going. Just 'out of here for ever'. One thing was certain, from what Ollie had said. No way would her brother be calling on her.

Coming from most teenagers, 'Tell her to stay away from me' wouldn't amount to much. A shrug and a scowl, turned into words at random and due to be forgotten the same day. But not from her transparent brother, who meant every word he said. In the loo, taking the train back into London, Miranda found herself choking on sobs as a queue formed outside. Wept like a girl, she thought, dabbing cold water on her face in front of the grungy mirror while the movement of the train made her stagger. Like it or not, that was surely all she was.

Twenty

The noise was the worst thing. Maybe the others thought it good form to shout a response, the way you're supposed to at a Christmas pantomime. Making believe they weren't all just watching a row of naked women at work. The dancers weren't that good anyway, despite the posh location. On Jack's initiative one late Saturday night Miranda and the others were in Soho, in a cellar between the showpiece office of a post-production company, and one of the West End's snobbiest vintners. If Jeanette had been there, she'd certainly have said something about crummy production values.

The men – boys once more, in this place – all made the same yowling noises, as though attending a dodgy pagan ceremony. Jack and Rob yelled remarks of the open-wider sort. Thomas looked cheerful, like an uncle being a good sport; Richard was intense and full of false elation. The two other women there, from Jack's year at art college, looked uncertain and said nothing. You could see they wanted to seem entertained.

It got different after Rob shouted at one of the performers by name. You wouldn't think anyone could tell them apart, even after they'd swapped those huge trembling wigs for tasselled mortarboards. They still had make-up with sequins included, and eyes done to look like glittery dark moons, with a bead thing on the end of each false eyelash. Look closely and you could see that no one in this line-up was just plain gorgeous enough to dance alone. To do banal things with loofahs, even. That was in the act just before, featuring a fair-haired girl, maybe a Slav, whose naiad looks had nothing to do with the dull stuff that made up normal women; you couldn't even picture her with menstrual cramps. Not that her act was filled with magic. Halfway through, one leg cocked high as if inserting a cap, you could swear the girl had been asking a regular on the front tables if he'd had a good holiday.

But then Rob had recognised one of the chorus. Someone he – all of them – knew. Once you realised it was Frances, every gesture was obviously hers. Even the way she stood.

The others were sobered after that, especially Richard. In Miranda's entry year at St Ted's, he'd been one of the older students appointed to help the new entrants cope with everyday life. She wasn't surprised to see him suddenly look fraught: Frances had been in his group of first-years. Thereafter he was obviously hoping like hell that the place was too dark and crowded for someone on stage to recognize any audience member.

Afterwards Jack accepted an invitation from the manager, who it seemed he knew, and they all had free drinks while standing around at the deserted bar. Only Jack had anything much to say; he and the manager, a small Algerian guy, talked about the club. 'All my girls are nice girls,' the man said. He mentioned that he was also in the import/export business. It didn't seem polite to ask what he imported, just in case it was people and they'd been looking at some of the luckier ones.

Twenty-one

Frances

They'd all said the same thing at the Student Counsellor place. So I suppose they might have been right. 'Sit down together with the person who makes you sad or angry and talk things through with her.'

What they told me was, 'Agree on the best, most reasonable way you and your mother can both achieve forgiveness and be happy again.' It was the same with just about everything I've read. Like the squirm-making book by that Californian woman whose inspirational public meeting I went to: *Yes, Cinders, You Shall Have a Life!* Of course, she was no use.

'Sit down together and talk.' If only people knew. My mother screaming at Phil that he was the great mistake of her life. Him, the best father in the world. And afterwards, Phil asking me, 'What should I do? What does she really want?'

And when I said, 'No, Mum, please!' she started saying even worse things to me. In the end she'd left without a word. I know there was all that shouting. But couldn't she have said something else to me in the end? That can't just be it.

That was when Phil wept in my arms. Unbearable. There had to be something I could do.

To me he never used to be Phil; I'd always called him Dad. But I wasn't having any of that now. Even if he'd wanted it, I was damned if I'd call him that during any of what came next.

Apart from medicals I'd never been naked in front of a man. I didn't dare tell him that.

I'd always loved Phil. That's why I had that other thought, right through everything we did. What else can I do for him? What do I dare?

Afterwards I was grateful too. To Fate, I suppose. Just for the chance at long last to show I was good for something.

Oh, but I make him so happy. Right away he was pleased with his life.

He started taking me out. To show me off, was what he said. He kept telling me, 'You know I've always been proud of you.'

We kept running into people Phil had known through work. One new thing: whenever he introduced me he was very formal. I know it was out of respect for me. But maybe acting so correctly in front of other people excited him too. I don't blame him for it.

Some of them had left the police as well, to play golf or set up a consultancy. But I know he regretted taking early retirement. Often with other people he couldn't help acting as though he had something to prove. Laughing too much, and interrupting when he shouldn't.

The worst point was when we found there wouldn't be enough money to set up the agency, for security services.

One thing made me specially grateful to him: for as long as he could, he tried to hide all that from me. Including the payment he'd had to make as part of the settlement. It was only when he talked about selling his car that I realized something bad had happened.

I know it was because of me. Of course he insisted it wasn't. Just as he'd always tried to stand between me and poor Mother's misery-guts rages.

To help somehow, I looked for paid work; not that I was much use at first. I heard about the dancing job while doing telephone sex. Two dozen of us in rows, mostly single mothers, talking dirty while out of their minds at leaving young kids on their own. I was hopeless of course, even though mostly you just had to listen. After that the club was a relief; you need so little talent it's almost impossible to be no good. That's one of the benefits. Along with making a proper financial contribution.

On stage I'm free to think about all sorts of things. Like, if Mother could see me now. Asserting myself. Making a public declaration. It's a way of saying, if anything's my fault, this is me showing I'm sorry – and what's more, I bet no one could do more than this to make things better.

Phil knows that. The day I got my first pay-check from the club. 'You're a great girl,' he said. 'You know that, don't you? You're a real trouper.' I know he can't always express himself the way he might like. Let's face it, if he could just hear how he sounds sometimes. But he means nothing but good, and I'll always respect and love him for that.

SUE WEBB

*

From the files of Makepeace and Maw, Solicitors

Subject: F65/B321-002

Last Thursday night was a delight for us too. Spouse says he hasn't had such an evening of it since the last time both of you pitched up chez nous.

On the latest revelation concerning the above case, this is by way of a shared File Note, the reason being that you may not care to be taken by surprise when the latest development is seen to burst upon us.

This client, as you know, has laid out no end of initiative in the interests of a more considerable settlement. You too, indeed, will have noted the client's response when reminded, however obliquely, that she's the disadvantaged party, being seen, fairly enough if you ask me, as the one who bolted.

There is issue, viz. 1 daughter. Even allowing for the costs of getting through med school, at twenty-two years of age said offspring might not be seen as much of a factor in this case.

Until now. Think what we may of our client's insistence on her case as 'a matter of principle', it has to be said that her efforts have now turned up something rather substantial.

What I mean is no less than an ardent carnal encounter, often several times per diem according to our client's professional source, between the respondent and his very own aforementioned stepdaughter.

After so many seemingly vain endeavours our client is now in all likelihood spot on when she describes the respondent as about to be stuffed at both ends like a spitted pig.

For us it is of course a notable victory. Though make of that what we will, in other terms. I mean, once one is in a position to communicate further …

Twenty-two

Miranda walked the last few yards to the mews flat in a fog. Not literally of course: it was high summer, the temperatures notorious across Europe, with no one on the street caring what rolls or swags of flesh they bared. Upper Street was a ragtime discord of food smells versus traffic fumes, its pavements greasy in a way that suggested they'd only get clean if the sky rained detergent suds for a week.

She arrived in the mews at her mirror-bright black front door and put down her bags of groceries. Took out her key. Went to put it in the lock. Then she heard footsteps inside. More than one person, and heavy enough to be male. But not hasty, as though a Fagin mob of underage youths was about to explode onto the street. She stood back, waiting for the door to open. Two youngish men came out. They carried an impressive amount of photographic kit. Tripods; a bundle that must be one of those umbrella things used as a reflector; and surely enough lighting for an operating theatre.

'Hi', she said. And felt a prat when acknowledged with a non-committal stare. Another man followed; a different breed altogether. He obviously worked out; his tousled hair was expensively cut; and he had the unreal good looks of a comic-book hero. He looked friendly, as if already introduced, and as he held the door open for her he zapped Miranda with a thousand-watt smile.

Upstairs she heard the new power shower. It was state-of-the-market, so while it lasted even shouting hello at Frances was futile. She went straight to get supper started.

'Oh!' Frances had come to the door of the neat little galley kitchen. She wore a huge white towel, with another around her head.

It wasn't like her to show surprise. Embarrassment, yes: any time. But not this bald show of dismay.

'I thought you started that job today.'

'They'd fired me before I got there.' Waiting on tables at the Seraglio, by the Green. Miranda had been kidding herself, thinking she could get there in time from St Edmund's. 'Maybe I should have walked if I wanted to beat the rush hour.'

She started unpacking onions and new potatoes into the carousel, and waited to hear about the men who'd just left. Frances was loitering, as though uncertain whether to say something.

Then Miranda turned on some fierce ceiling lights and Frances backed off. Even so Miranda couldn't miss it. Taking the towel off her head Frances wrapped it clumsily round her neck. She shook her wet hair loose around her face; then made a show of shading her eyes.

Miranda turned the lights back off. Without the sharp chaos of shadows they'd cast, she could actually see her friend's face much better. It was mottled, like the complexion of an angered old woman. At first she hoped Frances' pinpoint pupils were a response to the kitchen's film-studio brightness. But no.

With a terrible sense of misplacement, like a patient waking too soon, she knew. What Frances' towel hid had been a line of discoloration flaring round her neck.

She looked straight back at Miranda, transparent as always. Regardless of what her physical condition must have been a few minutes ago, she didn't look shaken at all.

'It's all right,' she said, with an almost-smile. 'I don't do stranglings just when anyone makes me. It's all properly negotiated.'

'Uh, right.' Even with her friend, God help her, Miranda's idiotic first impulse was to try and look supercool.

She turned back, making a business of filling the carousel with economy-sized bags of pasta. 'At least med school means you're properly qualified for stuff like that. Even if not officially. So to speak.'

'I hope you won't worry.' In her pleasant contralto, Frances could have been talking about going out in bad weather with no umbrella. 'You wouldn't believe how genteel it really is. The worst drawback is the number of towels I seem to be taking to the launderette. And I don't usually work from here. Honestly.'

'Yes ...' Miranda was thinking of how you'd look, being filmed like that. Physically gruesome once your breath was stopped up. Compared to which it was nothing if meanwhile someone rogered you. Presumably that *was* the job of the guy with the megawatt smile. With hindsight he seemed like an android, branded somewhere discreet with the words 'Stallion Man: Class A'.

An urgent question was forming in her mind. Then it clicked home, unwelcome as a roulette wheel giving the wrong result.

'But of course you're legal, aren't you?' It amazed her that Frances might be trimming right up to the edge of the law. The one thing everybody knew at med school was, one strike and you'll never practise. If you got indicted – for anything, crimes you'd think went out with being put in the stocks – the one thing you were bound to lose was your right to qualify.

Frances smiled again, evasive but not flustered. Was she just taking the least futile route for any student with not enough funding? The one that magically stopped all debts from consuming her like a chronic illness?

'You know how well organized I am.' Towelling her hair, she paused, with an habitual gesture of modesty, to hitch the bathsheet tighter. In her usual tone of good-natured mockery, she added, 'This is a proper business, you know. With ace filing and everything.' She indicated her computer, on its triangular kneehole desk that fitted so neatly into a corner of the sitting room. 'And don't worry: I do it hooded. All part of their make-believe narrative.'

After Frances had left to get dressed, Miranda went and sat for some time on the edge of her bed.

She should have noticed. Now she thought about it, a lot of Frances' energies had taken a new direction. Time at home would once have been spent on things like de-fragmenting her class notes on a vast hard drive. But recently she'd given her all to so-called personal grooming: the whole drudgery of pedicures and dry scrubs and weekly visits to the hairdresser. Now that she understood, nothing could have been more obvious.

For the first time since she'd known her, Miranda was angry. Well, apprehensive. Of all the possibilities whirling through her head – some fantastical, others just over-imagined – one absurd and horrible fact stood out.

By living here she herself faced a risk. Worse, the part of her in danger was the one she'd hoped and toiled for the most; for which she'd dreamed, impatient for the future. Her virtue-filled, splendid career.

With two of them at this address could they be charged with keeping a brothel? Here in Miranda's tiny room with its dirty-linen pile and a slurry of books and papers? Amid their banal domesticity such a notion seemed crazy. How could anyone interpret this little inner-suburban flat, fudged together over some former stabling, as a sanctum consecrated to forbidden pleasures?

But once her options had sharpened into perspective, they were clear enough.

Time to split once more.

Twenty-three

The frame, densely scrolled, held nothing but a giant question mark. To Etta it could have been a sentient eye staring out from her VDU. She bayoneted it with a look of purpose and waited.

No longer did she log on just in passing, before the day's main business. The PC now stood well away from the front door, in a former maids' room at the furthest end of the flat. In much the same way the building's first inhabitants had happily accepted the etiquette of keeping their electric telephone inside a cupboard. For Etta one's new home was for serious entertaining, not confronting guests with the clutter of daily life. She now lived in a grandiose Edwardian block with theatrically curving stairs and a great deal of marble and burnished mahogany; outside lay the tree-shaded Regents Park Canal with its passing boats full of corporate diners. It followed that she had definite views on what people were to note whom she invited there under her high ceilings.

But it was the early-morning check on her computer, in its corner where the cleaner wasn't to bother, that had become the day's important destination. So much the worse that for several weeks she'd logged on in vain, wasting irreplaceable minutes each day in a state of dread. How could her unknown enemy, this bloody person, be taking so long to follow up?

This time a new attachment showed. At first the same carpet as before, the same litter of clothes, the same bed. Etta strove to believe that nothing she'd seen so far could make life difficult. Anyone's computer could fill up with anonymous pornography sent at random. And surely so far none of these emails had anything to do with her. Really, she might perfectly well open them where any sort of people could sneak a look. At City Hall indeed, where Etta's progress through Public Relations had secured her a spacious office near the building's summit. And still there'd be no harm.

The same big carved bed with the same blurry, anonymous bodies filled most of the screen. Once more the sitar riffs were poorly dubbed over sex enacted as a series of tableaux, athletic trufflings you might see on contraband Victorian postcards. And still the couple's heads were hidden by the deep tasselled curtain.

The music stopped. The screen blanked out. Then a caption came up: Gothic typography, bristling with serifs.

'WHATEVER NEXT?'

Then another caption: 'MORE MOVING PICTURES?' Followed by: 'THEN PREPARE TO BE MOVED.'

And now a dark screen, with a new soundtrack. Voices only, this time. A mercy perhaps, that Etta still couldn't quite hear what was actually being said…

'But you mustn't touch me.' The woman.

Now the couple, still naked, were at another beginning. Their movements were tentative, slow as waterweed in a near-invisible current; their murmurings too low to convey meaning. From him, careful, slow-burning ardour. From her a show of modest reluctance.

Role-playing. A simulated seduction. Minutes passed while the woman shyly pushed away his hands...like this...but now... The camerawork was feeble and hard to read; even so, it was obvious when he grew stiff as a girder. There was an undertow of strung-out laughter as they struggled to keep up the original pretence. The woman's voice rose, tight with anticipation.

'Oh, all right, you great dick. Only, this is just one of those tantric thingys. It's like, just a spiritual thing. You needn't think I've really got you right inside me... We mustn't move. Except for both of us to breathe, really slowly. This is... it's a mental exercise...'

The phone rang at Etta's elbow. As she answered, she wasn't even conscious of snatching with her other hand at volume control.

'Right away,' she told the taxi driver taking her to work. 'No, wait—' striving to guess what else the screen would show – 'I'll need ten minutes.'

On the silenced VDU the man was poised to arch himself downwards into the woman's long, pale fake-passive body. As briskly as she'd killed the sound, Etta turned it up, in time to hear at least his moan of deliverance on entering.

Breathily the woman said, 'I know you think we shouldn't do this.'

For answer he started slowly moving back and forth on her.

'But,' she added, 'it's still all right, isn't it? If... all I need is go like... "Don't. Stop."'

No chance of that.

This time when the phone rang, Etta jumped – even reached out – then realized the sound came not from a distant room but from the recording. With the woman now on top, the couple froze – but only in the sense that the film did. With every pixel locked solid, the final image was hard to read. There was nothing to show whether the man was actually reaching down to the floor for the phone. Much less if, while he took the call, the woman would still service him.

Whatever Etta half-expected to see, she wasn't there yet.

Twenty-four

There'd never been so much sunburned gooseflesh. For once it was raining. Not just drizzle from a hot dark sky, the kind that evaporates as it reaches the pavement. There were puddles forming, so that you had to remember not to get splashed by traffic. And nobody minded – or maybe no one believed the weather could have changed, even for a day – as they commuted home with draggled hair or wet slashes down their shirt.

Miranda was edging along the pavement by the local Tube. In front of her she held an empty suitcase, narrow side first like a prow, as a shield against getting bumped into. It was nearly six o'clock and the oncoming crowds were being carried along by their own weight. The cool, strange-feeling rain had started making runnels under her shirt collar, back and front, and she could taste it on her mouth. Just before the Tube entrance, where a couple of newsstands funnelled passers-by almost to a standstill, she heard someone in a car call her name.

It was Richard in his bashed old Vauxhall, leaning across to the passenger window and shouting past the kerb-side railings to offer a lift. By the time she'd struggled to the crossing and got in, the traffic was backed up and hooting. It was no place for standing in the road and talking, so they were already whirling away like a leaf on a stream before he could tell her that, no, the mews flat could just as well be on his way.

She was going there to pick up the last of her stuff. For the next few weeks she'd actually been offered free lodging, by a classmate at St Ted's named Gopika. For the duration of Gopika's time in London her family in Chennai had bought her a tiny service flat in an ugly, well-appointed block off the Cromwell Road. It would shortly be resold along with its expensive furniture; her parents now wanted her to go home and get married.

They drove for a while in silence to the clunk of the windscreen wipers. With the rain streaming off every surface people outside looked like creatures in an aquarium.

'What are you thinking about?'

Richard's question surprised her. They'd only been friends, after all, rather than intimates.

'My brother.' She blurted a version of her visit to Josh's school, trying to make everything sound better than it was. Right now she didn't know if she wanted to find Josh and apologise, or do the childish thing and hide away till someone told her things weren't too bad.

Richard slowed to let two women with baby buggies cross the road, both leaning into the rain like figures on a frieze. The plastic cover over each buggy was opaque with condensation.

'What about the school?'

'All Adam said was, "We've sorted things out with them." He wasn't too clear what he meant. I would've gone back there but the holidays have started. So if any of Josh's friends have got news of him, I'll have to track them down one by one.'

'Are you sure your brother wants to be found just yet?'

This too she hadn't expected to hear. She'd seen Richard as an agreeable twerp, forgetting that psychiatry was his first and only ambition.

'Maybe not. But I think in his place I'd still like my family to be looking for me.'

'I'm sure your brother's all right.'

'But even if he is safe somewhere, I still need to look for him.'

'Look for him?' Richard said, emphasizing the first word.

'And find him too.'

*

Richard said he'd come in with her, to help carry things. Miranda would remember afterwards, as if having seen the place for the first time, how the little street resembled a stage set. The rain had stopped and a coppery sun struck reflections off west-facing windows. People were coming back out of the pub at the far end, drink in hand, like a chorus about to open Act One of some classical opera. A half-dozen pigeons clattered up into a shaft of sunlight as she went to open the front door.

Inside what took her by surprise was a blast of

nostalgia. Not for this particular place, where she'd lived scarcely any time, but for what its smell of fresh flowers and beeswax polish called to mind. Home, of course: a place of perfect order.

She was there to pick up all sorts: bulky stuff for winter, and a pile of back numbers from *The New England Journal of Medicine* that she wouldn't know were needed until she'd read them. Plus a jiffy bag she'd been meaning to deposit with her bank, holding the small number of letters Laura had written to her. The closer the relationship and the more you live in the same home, the fewer mementoes you're likely to have. There was also a photo album: Laura's childhood, then her own.

Richard carried the last two boxes, containing books and other home-office stuff, down to the car; she put on the kettle. It seemed all right to help themselves to instant coffee, in a friend's home, though not being a tenant any more made her reluctant to loot the real stuff and start grinding beans.

Coming back, Richard paused to look around. He'd never been here for more than a few moments and surveyed the place with a look of curiosity rewarded, like a well-read tourist.

'Hey, Mandy, look at this!'

'What?' She stared around, seeing nothing in particular; for an instant she expected some problem. 'Oh – yes, that's so like Frances.'

He meant how precisely Frances had organized her books. 'Cataloguing everything by all these languages' – there were at least four – 'and only then by subject. On some alternative world she must be a librarian.'

You Said She's Where?

'But a very senior one.'

'The Imperial Head Scribe of a national collection.' He went on examining Frances' books, craning upwards for a better view of the top shelf. Then, glancing towards Miranda, he said, 'Do you think she feels isolated at St Ted's?'

She fenced, not wanting to mention Frances' new livelihood. 'You don't mean by doing that job of hers. At the club?'

Richard actually blushed. 'I suppose so. She hasn't been around much recently.'

'True. Though she's always preferred to learn stuff by lurking in the library.' Instead of all the more chaotic and immediate ways of finding things out at the hospital.

'Do you think she prefers living on her own?'

Miranda wasn't sure, and said so. 'Besides,' she hedged, 'I couldn't afford to stay.'

Ever after, she couldn't believe that what happened next was unheralded. With hindsight the whole thing – absent-minded gossip, making coffee – carried their own horror. As if the place itself knew. Or Frances was watching close by.

The kettle shuddered to boiling point and clicked off. Richard closed a book he'd been reading and put it back on the shelf.

He said, 'I'm sure it's all right if I use the loo.'

'Fine. Coffee?'

'Thanks. Milk, no sugar.'

Alone, she reached for a couple of mugs. Then remembered she hadn't yet taken away a birthday present that Josh had given her as a curiosity. A coronation mug from 1936, showing the imminent ex-King, Edward VIII.

It was nowhere in the kitchen, which was tidy as ever and easily scanned. To the sound of flushing water from the bathroom, she looked around the sitting room to see if it had strayed.

Went towards Frances' room. Opened the door. Stood there. And stayed like that.

But she's changed it in here, was Miranda's idiotic first thought. Half a long, long second later and there was no fooling herself.

She made out the worst of it obscurely, like looking in a maze of distorting mirrors. The bedroom had been refurbished to look like a luxurious tent. A looped semi-transparent curtain hid most of it from the doorway, no doubt to give the illusion of being cut off from the world. But there was no mistaking a particular shape just above eye height.

A limp pair of shoulders and a crooked head. A pair of bare feet below the swag of drapery, toes pointing downwards, an inch above the floor. The nails had been varnished in pale pink like baby Venus shells, though the flesh beneath would have turned that shade of mauve long before she'd stopped breathing.

Miranda's first, obstinate thought was that none of this was to do with her friend. Frances wore a horrible fake-satin peekaboo bra in pink and black with matching panties, the crotchless kind that put you in mind of a defaced poster. Both were trimmed with pink swansdown.

Then, rage. The insult of being dead while wearing this whimsical tat. However disfigured by a slow, choking death, full nakedness would at least have been decently anonymous; little more than leaving the world as you entered it. Shame washed over her at how Frances must have suffered her last feeble convulsions while tricked out to suit some customer's silly dull fantasy.

Stupidly she thought, But Frances wasn't even allowed to die as herself.

*

She didn't have to die. That's what I thought at first.

It only came to me at the last moment that this was the right thing. The proper course. A perfect fit with events as they're meant to be.

All for the best. How often can you say that? She wanted to die anyway. She may not have known it, but it's true. Anyone can tell who knows about these things. She ought to have been grateful. The way she would have if she'd been sensible and known what she really wanted. Not that there was anything by then to stop destiny taking its course.

It was best to leave her dressed in that stuff. Like a cartoon pig. It'll give them something extra to argue about while they ask themselves, was she a fantasist as well as depressive?

And in the meantime. You don't go too fast, with something like this. You wouldn't want to get it wrong and hurry the next thing so that it's over in days. But what a calling card this was! The best yet.

SUE WEBB

Improvisation – everyone knows that's the key. Plans are for amateurs.

Twenty-five

'Some padding for you. After all that waiting around.' Richard passed a plate of toasted cheese.

It was late. When they were through with the police interviews, Miranda had told Richard, yes, tonight she didn't care to go home on her own. So here they both were, snacking in her latest flat's small, luxuriously furnished sitting room.

She couldn't eat though. Her mouth was dry, her eyes hot and scoured by fatigue. The whole of her face felt distended by tears. She put the smallest possible corner of toast in her mouth and slowly bit it off. Feeling queasy.

'Perhaps alcoholic hunger would help.' He got up and went into the tiny kitchen. 'Too bad you've no brandy. But at least I've found this,' he said, coming back with an unopened bottle of wine.' He poured some and handed it. Like everything in Gopika's flat it looked more expensive than anything you'd expect in a student lodging.

She took it and sipped. A vast ache had settled on her, a heavy not-feeling that suggested worse to come. It surprised her that she had almost no appetite for drink either.

Miranda had been glad at first that they were kept so long at the police station. She wanted to be shown that Frances was being taken seriously, without the smallest procedure being skimped. But how she'd talked and talked at the man and woman who'd interviewed her. And about nothing, for God's sake. Why should they care about the daily routines of sharing their flat? 'Only trying to help' must be words the police learn to dread.

Foul play. She wouldn't have been squeamish about saying the words; she just wanted the police to say them first. Otherwise they might think she was being overwrought. Self-important, even. She needed these people to think the worst, given everything else. The dissection-room hand. The texted threat while airborne.

At first she'd taken it for granted that was how they'd see Frances' death. After all there'd seemed no limit to the swirl of people and equipment appearing at the mews in response to Richard's call. When they began questioning her it still seemed to lead that way.

Had Frances had any enemies?

'None. Absolutely. Most people find they're disliked by someone, but she was different.'

'What about boyfriends?' Most questions came from the more senior of the two, who'd introduced himself as Detective Inspector Leese. A big man, whose movements were few and deliberate. Miranda recognized the woman from before: DC Rosa Hill, who'd called at the flat on the night Alicia found the severed hand. She'd done most of the questioning there; this time she sat and looked on, an attentive junior with things to learn.

'Do you just mean, did she have boyfriends – a boyfriend – and who were they?' Miranda was stalling, clumsily. 'Or, did she have a boyfriend she'd quarrelled with? In either case, I honestly don't know of anyone.'

She was damned if she'd shop her friend as a whore. Or even an erotic artiste courageously paying her way through med school as best she could.

And did Leese know already what business Frances had been doing, in the mews flat?

He said, 'You must have been living fairly cheek by jowl with Miss Brooke.'

'Well, it's a small flat. But I wasn't there for long.'

'Even in that time, you can't have had many secrets from each other.'

'I'm not sure. I mean, it's as though you're asking me to list every detail about which I know nothing. Including the fact that such details actually exist.'

He crossed his legs and resettled himself in his chair like a man whose reserves of patience were immeasurable. 'You stated that you saw the body. Close up.'

She nodded, finding she couldn't speak just at that moment.

'Therefore you must have observed Miss Brooke's clothing. Such as it was.'

'With respect, that may not be the case.' Rosa Hill looked at Miranda as she spoke, though she seemed concerned only to be heard by Leese.

'Exactly,' Miranda put in. 'I could say I saw only the evidence of trauma caused by strangulation. Though as it happened I did take in what she – Frances – was wearing. Sort of noticed,' she added, trying not to sound defensive.

'Someone in your position can't pretend they've never seen the effects of violent death before. By now you must have served the usual time in A & E?'

'I was on duty during the Hollis Green crash,' she said, certain that something so dire must have involved him too. It was men and women from this station, among others, who'd had to work their way through a blood-soused railway carriage shrilling with ownerless phones. 'But I don't recall noticing the details of anyone's underwear.'

Leese gave her a heavy look and turned to DC Hill. 'You wanted to make a point?' She shook her head and looked down at her hands.

Miranda said, 'Look, Frances really was a private sort of person. But she was very organized in all the details of her life. And she always expressed herself in a totally straightforward way.'

'Meaning?'

She let herself sigh; she couldn't help it. They'd been in here for an hour and it was nearly midnight. Was Richard still being questioned? Or was he no longer in the building?

'Maybe she had no secrets at all. Perhaps this was done to her at random. And besides—'

Suddenly, bent forward, she found herself mouthing in silence. Caught short. Miranda felt like a pair of bellows that wouldn't work. She wasn't lost for words, just the power of speech. In marathon running they speak of 'the Wall', the invisible barrier several miles in that gives no warning it's there. That's where she'd just arrived.

Both of them looked on, struck dumb though she was, with all the close professional attention she could have wished. She clasped her head, then raised a hand, gesturing for them to wait. There was a long silence. Then, 'Besides,' she resumed, breathing out hard, 'was it meant to be her?'

Miranda recognized her own training in the response this got. Both went on looking at her but were careful to say nothing.

'Any threats I know about were made to me, not her. You were there,' turning to Rosa Hill. Miranda was pleading – imploring – and she despised herself for it. But part of her was too angry and frightened to care. 'You were there, when someone left me… that hand.'

She chanced a look at Leese to check his response. If he didn't know what Miranda was talking about he gave nothing away.

'And I got another threat, a text, only I couldn't show anyone because I dropped the damn phone and lost it.'

Leese said, 'So what was the threat you received? Before we go any further. Can you tell us the exact wording?'

Miranda stared up at a corner of the room as she replied, to avoid looking at him. The ceiling must have been lowered, to create a space for ducts and cabling. Leese's face wore the look of a man who was giving his all to finding out the truth and didn't deserve to be disappointed.

'Someone called me up while I was paragliding. I was several hundred feet up. I accidentally dropped the phone. So I can't remember every word, only the tone of what was said.'

He leaned forward. 'But Miranda. You just said you received a threatening message. How exactly was it worded?'

And that was that. She didn't rise to her feet and sweep out, with a look of disdain at the stupidity of his question. Nor did she shout, nor murmur a syllable of protest. She did the one thing she'd meant not to, and wept. Noisily, streaming snot as wetly as if something major had ruptured. All the grief, all the rage, all the uncertainty and fear were now in the service of a frustration that shook her physically, with the violence she'd like to have shown Leese right then.

She was deftly escorted out, sobbing raucously, standard background noise for a large metropolitan police station. The daftest things, it seemed, go through your mind when you're beside yourself, possessed by two streams of consciousness at once. All the while, making her way hunched up and noisy through the reception area, she found herself thinking how this building, with its strip lighting full of dead flies and its polystyrene ceilings, was indistinguishable from most of St Edmund's. Only, whereabouts here would you expect to find anything like the dignified murals by Jack's great-uncle? And if you could, what might they show? Famous arrests with everyone posed like a classical relief? Statuesque stakeouts? In reception the roof had been leaking, so she had to sit and wait in a Portakabin replacement, she with face uplifted and streaming and Rosa Hill trying to hide her desire for Richard to appear and take Miranda away.

You Said She's Where?

*

Gallantry, as survivors from Kitty's generation called it, has many forms. Given responsibility for an incurably weeping woman, many guys of Richard's age would offer embraces and murmurs of encouragement. A few, openly uneasy, might stick to offering tissues and holding doors open. He responded as he'd done in the mews when he'd made Miranda walk downstairs and out into the late sunlight, to sit in his car while he made the first call. Rather than clasp her by the elbow or put an arm round her shoulders, he was careful to avoid any touching. In its way it was a chivalric gesture, one that meant not to take advantage. Some people learn good behaviour towards the frail, the young, the stricken. Others at least find ways to imitate it. But people like Richard evidently behaved well because no alternative could occur to them.

In the flat, collapsed on its big sofa, Miranda still found a sob rise up every so often, like a colossal air-bubble from a submerged wreck. She knocked back the glass of wine Richard gave her without relishing any part of its progress into her stomach. But held her glass out anyway for a refill.

'I don't want to talk about Frances any more. Even though I can't think about anything else.' Speaking of a friend newly dead counted on any terms as an act of mourning. And doing that was not something you did properly when senseless with fatigue.

'What do you want to do?' He looked calm but alert, as if there weren't any answer he'd expect. Yes, he really should make a good psychiatrist.

There was no sidestepping this moment.

'I want to lie down in bed with you and let things take their course. Even if it just means falling asleep right away and not waking up all weekend.'

There was no lingering, with something as easy and inevitable as this. They didn't even look at each other, in the ghostly pre-dawn light, until they were in the bed.

'Do you want to sleep?' His voice was thicker than he must have meant it to be.

'No! I mean… no.'

Nothing, and everything, was surprising – and as ordinary and needful as taking the next breath. One of those times when the invisible god of fucking stands right there, daring you to give her/him a straight look.

At one moment, just how you'd yearned for, she couldn't go on bearing it. Then she was asleep. Sensationless, as if profoundly anaesthetised.

Twenty-six

Thank God it wasn't winter. An evening of warmth and light with windows open to the sounds of traffic made this latest home like starting a foreign holiday. In January, coming in with steaming breath and no idea where to find the light switches, maybe then you'd feel more like a displaced person on the run.

Most people, however transient, see one thing as the centre of their home. The telly facing a deep beer-stained sofa. The comfortable bed with a disordered nest of opened books beside it. The big table in a kitchen that always held some warmth overnight. For Miranda it was logging on and being absorbed into whatever was on the screen.

Tonight, despite most of her stuff not unpacked, she'd have to work, reading up the notes on one of 'her' patients: a teenager due for a thyroidectomy, who'd wept to hear of having the base of her throat cut wide and pulled open. Waiting for the start-up screen, she murmured with impatience even though it flowered into view sooner than you'd take to cross the room.

Her phone sounded from the depths of her work bag. She jumped, then wondered irrationally who could see her sitting near the window. No matter that across the street were just the businesses you'd expect round here. A shop dealing only in olive oils; a florist selling indoor trees; Kensington's foremost balti restaurant. Most of their upstairs windows were empty; the others hidden by blinds. One had polyester curtains in a fake leopard-skin print, and a window box planted with plastic blue tulips; what Josh, half admiringly, would call High Terrible. Maybe inside was a sofa upholstered with lime green shag, like a great nylon-furred Afghan hound in need of a bath.

'Is this a good time?' a voice said at the other end. A man. 'Miranda? That is Miranda, isn't it?'

The voice didn't suggest a stalker. No underhand malice; nothing triumphant or insinuating. Rather, this was someone used to plain dealing and authority.

'You'll need to know that my name is Phil Brooke; Frances' – I mean, we met briefly at Frances' flat. Look, I need – there are things you and I should talk about. Face to face.' For politeness' sake there was a question in his voice.

Also, did he sound faintly unnerved? He added, 'Would you be free now?'

Was this her chance to be heard by someone who could get things done? She started to say, 'Well, yes—' but he cut her short.

'If you don't mind? Maybe later tonight, if now isn't a good time?'

His urgency almost made her want to hold him off. In the end she agreed to meet him here in the flat. Tomorrow, before she left for the hospital.

Ringing off, for half a minute she stared at the VDU. She'd wanted to offer him some verbal remembrance of Frances. But the moment and the words had evaded her.

Too abstracted at first, she saw but didn't perceive. Then—

This was the wrong screen. These file names weren't hers. Let alone the cache of memory sticks pouched up inside the laptop case.

Frustration was the first thing she felt, like a massive physical impact. She shouted a tedious series of obscenities, then put her elbows on the desk and sunk her head in her hands. After a length of time she couldn't afford to waste, she looked up again at the screen.

Or were these her files? Several icons surely had names given by her, even if their places on the start-up screen were changed. She felt a pang of hope. Maybe a world did exist where tomorrow she'd have got safely past the morning's ward round.

Then came a moment that prickled her with panic. Maybe some of these *had* been her files. But who'd put the others there? One horrible answer offered itself.

Why had she believed that the stalker... whatever... would sooner or later lose interest and just leave her alone? Defeat took hold of her, first as a dull ache of misery, then sharpening to a dread that drove out every other thought. If this laptop *was* hers, someone else – uninvited – must have reprogrammed it. Changed the files around, altered them, added things, from no motive but malevolence.

The screen looked back at her: a battle formation of evil eyes.

Then – Fool! Stupid, stupid cow! This laptop wasn't even hers – but that needn't be a problem. Hers was somewhere here, only under a pile of other stuff: so that was tomorrow sorted. Meanwhile this was – had to be – the one that had belonged to Frances. Her mistake was easily understood. It dated from a recent Sunday afternoon when several of them had come back from the pub for takeaway pizzas and pints of tea. While the others lounged around in the sitting room, reading the papers with barely room to turn a page, she and Frances had been in her bedroom, tinkering through an IT mind-dump. Trading lecture notes while Frances held forth about systems architecture.

That was why, for a paranoid instant, Miranda had thought this laptop was hers: all those file names they'd invented in common. Helping her move out, Richard must have picked up the wrong one.

She went over to her half-unpacked things and fumbled through until she found a clean memory stick. Unhesitating now, she sat back down at Frances' computer.

This time the start-up screen gleamed with reassurance. She went first to the in-box, to see what this might say about Frances' last few days.

In the event, there was nothing. Only two things stood out. Untypically Frances had failed to clear any recent junk mail; plus there was none of the gossipy, often in-jokey to-and-fro emailing that Miranda had always taken for granted. It was as though weeks had gone by, not hours, since her friend had ceased to exist.

All the more reason to see the address file. As she typed, it occurred to her to ask, could *he* be hiding here, in plain sight – Miranda's own 'secret admirer', as Detective Inspector Leese had chosen to describe him? And scrolling through – well, how was anyone to know? But at least this read the same as ever, being obsessive in its completeness. Each entry gave name, details of partners, present and recent; names of the few children born so far to any friends, with dates of birth. Also addresses, home and work, no extension number left out, and any other phone number all the way down to mobiles owned by next of kin.

Her own four last addresses were all given, with the extinct ones asterisked. For what it might be worth, she wiped the last two, along with four phone numbers and one email address. Futile or not, instinct still prompted her to banish any possible illusion that she too had been on the game.

Thank God meanwhile for some knowledge of how Frances' mind worked. Had worked…

They'd ended up sharing one or two types of password; names of lost villages was one. Miranda for her part had several fake addresses online, most featuring a settlement destroyed by the Black Death.

Would it save time if she tried guessing from memory? At her fifth attempt up came one such name: Ryme Extrinsica, in Dorset, wiped out *c.*1350. Some of the attached file names were also familiar.

Faces-U-Meet. Frances had had a taste for parodying anyone – advertising copywriters, Channel Five presenters, people met in real time – whom she'd found patronizing or ludicrous. Miranda clicked on it – then found it unexpectedly repurposed.

At random she read: Kevin the Caber … Tool-User Tom … Each was followed only by a mobile number. She paged down, reading at random. 'The Squire of Much Hadham', again followed only by a phone number. Plus several nicknames that looked more like introductory titles to some kind of narrative: 'Mr Seminary Man Shares a Tootle'; 'Rangefinder, Or, The Good Seed Guy'.

She clicked onto another file. 'Look, Mother!' the opening caption read, elaborately framed like the commentary to a silent movie.

But the corner of the frame held wording in another, spiky font. Almost imperceptible, like a murmured aside. It said, 'I dare you.'

The phone rang again.

'Miranda – Mandy?'

'Oh Richard!' It came out as a sigh. From relief at hearing him plus confusion at what she'd just sighted next. At the instant she picked up the phone the VDU had shone into focus on a bizarre tangle of highlights. Buttocks, kneecaps, bare soles of feet, like an intricately plaited loaf of bread warping and twitching.

'You sound…?'

Anything rather than say, 'I'm fine' when it was a flat lie. 'I'm drowning in it. Work, I mean.' As she spoke she tried to keep her eyes from sliding back to the screen. Everyone was wearing a mask, she realized. Maybe a wig as well.

'Can I come over?'

She remembered her rash promise to be here when Frances' stepfather called. 'If you can bear to sit and watch me panic.'

'I'll bring some takeaway.'

'Now you mention it you'll have to or we'd starve.' Talk of supper made it the sort of conversation old-established couples shared. Such ordinariness. Could anything be more welcome?

After Richard rang off she turned back to the screen and started on the only course of action that made sense. She needed to find out the contents of each document, then wipe anything from Frances' hard drive that shouldn't be seen. If she worked through to some drop-dead hour of night she could do it.

Everything she could, she put on a stick. In her panic she almost didn't stop to label its plastic pouch. Tomorrow Phil, as next of kin, would doubtless be in search of Frances' missing laptop. But if anyone was going to mistake their student flat-share for a bordello and finger her, Miranda was ready to do far worse than thieve her dead friend's correspondence.

Outside, the dusk smelled of hot tarmac overlaid with traffic fumes plus a dozen nationalities of restaurant. In half an hour Richard would be here. Miranda hunched towards the screen and scrolled on.

Twenty-seven

He actually glanced to either side before he came in. Closing the door she herself, in knickers and one of Richard's shirts, felt like Miss Sexually Compromised of 1930. Due for harsh looks from the neighbours if not a large badge marked F for fornication.

Richard was still sleeping. But Miranda had started into open-eyed consciousness a whole minute before Phil was due. He was on time to the second.

'I'm having coffee anyway,' she said, as she led the way into the narrow kitchen. Her throat felt like a desert riverbed this morning. She and Richard had ended by allowing themselves so little sleep, she almost expected the coffee to rasp on its way down.

Phil looked too much on edge to go and sit anywhere. Besides, the big sofa was only one internal wall from where Richard slept, his long legs scarcely covered by a tangled sheet. And on the sitting room floor Richard's jeans and sneakers, along with hers, were lying as though they'd been flung there during a burglary. The better to keep their voices down they stood in the narrow kitchen, each clasping a mug of instant, with the polished toes of Phil's shoes almost touching Miranda's bare feet.

It was good of her, he said, to let him come and see her like this. 'You do know that, don't you?' For emphasis he clasped her elbow. A schmoozer's gesture of intimacy, useful for almost any social occasion. Yet she could swear he didn't know he was doing it, even as she smelled the rush of his newly mouth-washed breath. His skin was grey and dry; his eyes almost the colour of conjunctivitis. It was obvious he'd been weeping.

Two personalities in one. The lecher and the inconsolable parent. Yet Frances had spoken of him with unconditional love. Maybe she'd always seen past his look of being up for it, with his natty motor and fussed-over clothes, straight through to someone capable of all-consuming grief.

'I always liked and admired her. I mean – I still do – always will.'

When people hear something hard to bear, they can visibly flinch. As though a shadow flits over them, so briefly that afterwards you think you saw nothing. That was what Frances' stepfather did now.

Then, just as suddenly, he gave her an automatic, purely sexual glance of assessment. It turned her hot with anxiety, standing there on the chilly tiled floor in the blue and primrose light of sunrise. Backed up against the controls on the oven, all she knew was that she was anxious for him to say what he wanted and leave.

She drank the coffee too fast, scalding herself. Was the silence that followed meant to make her babble? As an interrogation technique it was corny enough, yet she responded anyway, blurting something about being glad to help with returning Frances' computer. Of course that was why he was there. He said as much – then hastened to change the subject.

'You were close, weren't you? As in really good friends?' He looked at her, steadily.

'Oh, yes! I mean Frances always told me everything. No, I'm sorry – that's a stupid thing to say. No one can be sure of that.' Miranda shifted her feet about on the cold floor. Couldn't he see her arms and legs were covered in goose bumps?

'So you don't know why she did what she did?'

Think carefully. He must be talking about suicide – mustn't he? Or could he know at least some of what his stepdaughter had been doing for money? She fell back on answering a question with a question.

'Look, have you talked to the people investigating this?' She tried to hold his bloodshot gaze, willing him to give a straight answer. 'I mean, when they interviewed me, no one seemed ready to rule out anything.'

'You mean, did they mention suicide?' Still the immovable questioning copper, he demanded, 'Did they – *did* they – suggest that for some reason she may have been depressed?'

She started to say something but he went straight on. 'Because, Miranda, if that was the reason, weren't you the person best placed to notice?'

'I know she was usually straightforward. That doesn't mean she wasn't self-contained as well.'

He put his nearly full mug to one side, unnoticing. 'I think I know what you're saying.'

'Do you?'

'Of course. Frances...' He stopped, looking perfectly collected. Like some people do when they can't speak right away and stay calm. At that moment his stony face made her pity him more than any tears. He went on, 'Frances wanted to be perfect, in everything she did. She shouldn't have pushed herself like that. All the time. It made her life too hard to bear.'

Miranda tried to ignore his grief, kept so steadfastly just out of sight. 'That's still not what I meant—'

'What, then?' Almost imperceptibly, he moved closer. She could feel the heat from his face.

'When we shared that flat—'

'Yes?' His look said: I'm giving you one chance to say the right thing. 'Well?'

She could never have guessed how quickly pity could be pushed aside by pure rage. Damn you! she thought. She said, 'Didn't she tell you?'

'What? Tell me what?'

'That I'd been threatened?'

'Threatened? Who by?'

'Oh, for God's sake!' Was everyone out to make her feel like a deranged fantasist? She paused, and carefully, slowly, beat her fist against the nearby work surface in time to several deep breaths.

'I'm sorry—' she began again. 'I'm sorry, I didn't mean to sound like that. Only...' Pause once more; another effort. 'Okay, well if you hadn't seen Frances recently, maybe she'd never told you.'

She chanced a look at him, but needn't have bothered: he wasn't saying a thing. In a clenched voice, not caring how she sounded, Miranda told him about every previous disquieting incident. When she'd finished, he seemed thoughtful. If he says something sympathetic or helpful, she told herself, just don't cry, okay?

At length he said, 'But you have told all this to Leese?' This time he didn't seem to be chasing a particular answer; he just wanted to know what had happened.

'Oh,' she sighed. 'Oh, yes!' She could feel the tension deflating out of her, ready to be replaced by relief.

'And what did he say?' There was no sympathy in his manner after all. Right away the risk of her breaking up in tears was banished.

'He didn't say anything much. Not even that I was being unduly imaginative.'

Seeing him look stonily attentive, Miranda no longer gave a damn what he thought of her; she was too angry. As though an airbag had exploded in her chest.

'I know,' he said. 'You're shocked; you're grieving. Tired out by every bad feeling. But that's not to fear even worse for Frances than what happened. Or feel guilty because this time she was depressed enough to kill herself.' He hesitated, then added, 'I knew her too. Believe me. I did understand her. You do accept that, don't you?'

She failed to meet his eyes, and he took that as agreement. 'Well,' he said. 'I shan't keep you.' Having made his point he was in a hurry to be gone. 'I've spoken to Leese, too. And one or two other people from my old job. Frances knew of lot of them personally – did you realise that?'

You Said She's Where?

Of course. It couldn't be that no one cared. Not when there were people on Frances' case who could have been his ex-colleagues; friends even. She felt her anger running down; soon it would dwindle to a dead weight and she'd be grateful just to crawl back into bed, tuck herself behind the curves of Richard's drowsing body, and stop wondering, just for a while, what she should think.

Leaving, Phil shook hands with an air of finality. 'That's that, then.' As in definitely no more questions. Especially from her.

Twenty-eight

For days Miranda's increasingly tatty copy of the Big Issue was something she'd carried everywhere. She'd been through every photo of Josh that Kitty said she could spare. Most of them she couldn't have faced sending to the magazine. It would have filled her with superstitious dismay to see him full of the glee of just being alive, here on the Missing Persons page.

In the end she'd chosen one where he looked inattentive. She was glad she couldn't remember when or where this picture had been taken. So often you could even recall what someone was saying when the camera had flashed and clicked. One had showed a gang of them boating near Stumblehurst, all sunburned legs and canvas shoes – she and Jeanette, Josh and his classmate Ollie Gunton – each raising a beer can towards the camera in a satirical toast to Thomas, who'd uncharacteristically run them aground in a reed bed on the narrow River Arun. In a photo from the same day, taken on the farmhouse lawn, they were posed and guying in ranks, with Thomas and the two boys on one knee in the front row like some po-faced record of a big-game hunt. Kitty, with her professional's instinct for portraiture, had snapped them when they'd been unprepared. Miranda could still hear the smile in Kitty's voice as she'd said, 'Serious attitudes, please. No one bare their teeth, even if they mean it agreeably.'

Some of the stories on the page now bearing Josh's image. In this edition the three other missing people smiled straight at you. One was a headmaster, or had been until he lost his job; another, the mother of two young children, had run an IT company. The third, a thirtyish man, had gone missing when on holiday in Cyprus with a group of friends. Their photos were all in colour, which made the quality vary far more than if they'd been ancient snaps in black and white. One man's features couldn't possibly have been so orange in real life; another looked as if photographed through a brown haze.

All this made it hard to believe, thank God, that these people had anything in common. Let alone the fact, wretched or terrible, of their disappearance. 'All his family and friends feel great concern for his safety.' 'Her children miss her terribly.' Surely they wouldn't all be found? And how many hundreds of others were there, just in London?

Could she face Josh yet? In his unprecedented rage? Yet she couldn't have done nothing. She'd placed the entry as a message; an apology. Whether he'd care or not. In the same way, she had to begin seeking him out. Starting at the likeliest place.

She put the magazine away. Richard was coming back to their table, in the brasserie near her flat. They'd been wolfing down a late Sunday brunch: roast red pepper quiche with anchovies, smoked salmon and goat cheese;

Buck's Fizz; fresh raspberry tartelettes. Last night had left them both light-headed.

'Let me give you a lift out there,' he said, when they emerged squinting onto the sunlit street. There'd been rain and now it was a proper summer's day, clear and fresh after the steamy tropical dullness of recent weeks.

'It could take some time.'

'You can't mind keeping me hanging around. When it's something like this.'

'Yes, I can.'

'I can do some work in the car.'

'Oh ... Richard.' It came out as a sigh. 'Please humour me.' Pretty, pretty please.

'You don't mean that?'

'I do.' She did, absolutely. Bad enough that she'd spent yet another night using this good man for her pleasure.

Also she didn't know what she might find, seeking news of Josh. If they did meet how would Josh respond? Would he even listen when she tried to make peace?

Parting at the bus stop she and Richard swapped a wordless smile; the careful farewell of new lovers not wanting to move ahead too fast. But looking back as the bus drew away she saw his features widen into a grin, then realized that was how she looked.

The bus wallowed down Park Lane. From the litter-strewn top deck everything today looked remote as a movie. At Hyde Park Corner they pulled up to let the Queen go by. She wore red – presumably the job obliged her to dress in a block of strong colour for the cameras – and was being driven across the roundabout where nobody

You Said She's Where?

goes, straight through the monumental arch at its centre. No doubt Her Majesty must get about as much as anyone. But this morning to Miranda it seemed a sleep-deprived hallucination to watch the royal Daimler, heraldic banner and all, gliding by like a little runaway banqueting hall.

Richard, though. Maybe it was for the best that he'd soon leave the country. On the Tube, then the Overground, watching the run-down suburbs flow past, she tried out several fantasies of what came next. Maybe the one that played best pictured a meeting with Richard twenty years on, both grateful for a carefree, long-ago relationship whose memory had put meat on their bones and helped them take the right steps onwards and elsewhere.

Fool, she thought, once these imaginings had spooled themselves out. She walked away from the station at Kingston and over the river. Stupid woman. What she'd done was seduce him. She'd been wretched and angry and scared and she'd used him to distract herself. And going back tonight to lie in that deep soft bed, his long legs entwined with hers? That was no way to make amends. But by the time she reached where Josh's boat was supposed to be, she knew that's what would happen.

The islet she was looking for lay down a track between high hedges. This was a world of sports grounds with clubhouses like country seats, and mansions with perfect lawns and a matching boathouse: pseudo-Tudor, Germanic baronial. The riverside near London was another country, where people brandished fantasies they'd never hint at elsewhere. A thatched roof incorporated a straw cat stalking along its ridge; a real stuffed camel looked down towards the water from a picture window; an elderly couple, as tweed-and-cashmere as rich old people from fifty years ago, took tea on their lawn in a medieval-style pavilion with its canvas opening scrolled back. Apart from the tourist traffic on the river, the only sound was a moorhen's croak or the splash of Canada geese touching down.

To cross to Pickerels Eyot you had to winch yourself over, on a pedestrian ferry not much bigger than a table top. Standing and turning a handle was like trespassing across some ducal moat. A path led between pre-war bungalows, each achingly neat with a fresh-painted wooden verandah, amid container gardens in Union Jack colours of geranium and lobelia. The place whiffed of briskly organized retirement. Every home stood on pillars of brick, for when the river rose in winter and came rilling over every garden.

Josh's boat wasn't always supposed to be here. It had lived at Stumblehurst, by a wonky little landing stage below the lawn. Adam had bought it on an impulse last year as a seventeenth-birthday present: a twenty-foot cabin cruiser, only two previous owners. Very few finishing touches had been necessary. Half a dozen tie-on fenders needed to be bought from a chandler's shop near Covent Garden, along with a new drinking-water tank; plus the canvas hood over the stern had to be replaced.

'Don't worry, Joshie,' his father had promised. 'You'll be able to mess about on it soon.'

Josh's delight nonetheless at this gift had made tears stand in his parents' eyes. By early last summer the boat had been made pristine and ready for days of timeless pleasure.

You Said She's Where?

Except that, one recent weekend, it wasn't there. Josh had responded with such dumb dismay that Miranda immediately started phoning round. Five calls later Wendy had informed her in neutral tones of embarrassment that, no, it hadn't been stolen, but moved away.

Where to?

The mooring on the Thames near Kingston was for safety's sake, Wendy had been told. Since the farmhouse was now empty. And made an excuse to ring off.

Josh's boat was in a row of moorings away from the main channel of the river. A couple of families were picnicking on the grass beside one cabin cruiser; nearby their children played swing-ball. On the boat next to Josh's a retired-looking man and his wife were swabbing and burnishing, much as some people clean their car every Sunday. As if pride of ownership was more important than setting sail for real.

She felt conspicuous arriving with none of the hampers or toolkits people brought to a place like this. A CCTV camera looked down from the trunk of a lofty swamp cypress; below, a carefully made notice declared, No Landing. Miranda started unfasting the stiff outsize poppers on the boat's canvas hood. It took an effort, so she didn't bother undoing more than necessary before it was possible to wriggle inside.

This little fibreglass cruiser had been Josh's most cherished possession; he too had regularly scrubbed or buffed every surface. At the least this was the first place to look; if he was living here some sign must be visible.

But not so easily interpreted. There was water still in

the tap, from the hefty plastic container under the sink. There were plates and cups and cutlery, tidied away and all mismatched like most people use on holiday. The food cupboard held its standing stock of olive oil, tinned tuna and white beans, plus a not quite empty carton of teabags. A plastic box contained a slab of Parmesan, hard as a geological sample.

Had Josh been squatting here? She didn't trust herself to guess. But there was no ignoring that there was no sleeping bag, nor any clothes stored under the lift-up seats in the prow. The claustrophobic shower cubicle, in which no one could ever stand upright, held a bar of soap, hard and dry, but nothing else. The tiny fridge was turned off. And a faint smell infested everything. Not the staleness of cobwebs and undisturbed dirt, but a whiff of recent corruption.

It came from the little pedal bin behind its curtain in the galley. There were two dried-out teabags, a baked-bean tin not yet mouldy, and an empty long-life milk carton still short of its use-by date. Josh had to have been here. Which meant someone from the lost world of this neat, inward-looking island must have seen him.

Before leaving, Miranda took out the Big Issue, folded open at Missing Persons, and scribbled a message in the margin. Then put it where it would be seen, anchored under a tin of olives.

She didn't make an apology, even though she'd come here to say sorry. You can't properly do that to anyone unless you're looking them in the eye. 'Dear Joshie,' she'd written, 'Everything here about you is true.' She meant especially the bit about herself, desperate for him to get in touch via St Edmund's. 'Please, please at least let me know that you've seen this…'

Getting out again was difficult. Only by standing on the rubbish bin could she slither out backwards through the gap between the edge of the boat and the canvas hood. Leaning half in and half out, she tried to free herself by undoing more poppers.

A tap on her shoulder. Anyone's fingers feel bony when they startle you like that.

'Are you sure you know what you're doing there?'

The man's voice was sharp with purpose, no friendliness intended. Getting free of the hood, Miranda stood on the ledge round the outside of the hull and jumped ashore, landing heavily on all fours. The man stood foursquare and watched her, his wife lingering a short distance behind.

She got back up and wiped the mud off her hands. 'I'm just—'

'Who are you?'

'My brother owns this boat. I'm—'

'We were told there might be squatters here. The Committee's been warned about people like that. On this boat.'

'This one?'

The wife came up to within a pace of her husband. They were dressed for an afternoon of serious refurbishment, in nylon boiler suits. 'One of the owners told the Committee we should look out. In case those people came back here.'

'What people?' And which owners?

The man said, 'Are you the person who rang?'

'No, actually,' Miranda said, trying to sound patrician as hell and not at all young. 'And there is only one owner. Did they give a name? Or an address?'

'You can't just come round here asking for people's addresses.'

Fair enough. She gave the Albany Square address, to see if it raised a sign of recognition. Getting no response she said, 'That's one of the places where my brother lives.' As a last resort she added, 'Except during term,' and gave the name of Josh's famous school.

They softened into a look of respect, making her feel like a cheat. People had no business being so easily impressed.

'Oh, they weren't anything like that,' the woman said. 'These weren't gentlemen at all.'

Miranda groped in vain for a mental picture of how this couple might see Josh as owner. A young fogey? With dialogue by P.G. Wodehouse? Maybe they thought he was a housemaster.

'You saw them?'

'Oh, we saw them all right. Three of them, there were. And they'd had the cheek to stay on your brother's boat all night.'

'Really?'

'They had an eyebrow ring—'

'One of them had a ring, pierced right through his eyebrow—'

'And there was one big one, with long ginger hair—'

'Dark ginger, which I'm sure looked as if he'd dyed it—'

'And they'd all got these baggy trousers, all ragged, with dirt round the bottom.'

Ollie Gunton, no doubt. With his brother Ralph as host creature to the eyebrow ring. And poor Joshie as the neighbourhood's other public enemy.

'I hate to think what kind of mess they left for you to find.'

Miranda wavered between looking sorrowful and reassuring. 'So then what happened?'

'Well, we told the Chairman of course. After we'd seen them leaving.'

'You could see him if you like, but he's not here today.' For people who valued belonging at any cost, this island had to be the perfect place. So long as you didn't mind leaving your privacy behind, like gunmen disarming themselves for church.

'So... do you know who it was that phoned – who called your, um, Chairman?'

The wife looked anxious, trying her best to help. 'Well, I think it was a woman. Maybe your brother's wife? Or a secretary? At the last meeting, someone did say it was a woman who'd arranged for the mooring. In fact – yes – it was Mrs Rawlinson who told me – the Chairman's wife. She said the woman who rang was really quite demanding when she asked about security. She obviously had your brother's best interests in mind. I know he can't have wanted youths like that coming round here.'

A pit of foreboding opened up in Miranda as Etta strode to mind. 'Did she – the woman who called – describe anyone in particular? When she mentioned keeping them away from the boat?'

'Oh, yes, definitely. I think your brother should be really grateful to have people like that on his side.'

Hearing of Etta's attempted sanctimonious theft rendered her wordless. She managed at length to say, how hateful. How totally illegal. How monstrous.

She avoided their indignant look of sympathy. By now, she figured, they were about to ask her in for tea; but given what she'd just found out Miranda didn't trust herself to be polite to anyone.

But they *had* been helpful. That much she did say.

Twenty-nine

'De-clutter!' people had said, the ones with an appetite for TV makeovers. And Miranda believed that on Kitty's behalf she'd actually done that. It seemed so easy at first. Just put everything interesting into storage – the valuable paintings and drawings and the piles of old hardbacks, many of them first editions, some signed. Thereafter, surely all she had to do was clean the place.

'I can see someone's done a lot of work,' the letting agent ventured after she'd looked around. 'Certainly enough for an expert eye to see a lot of potential here.'

'You mean the place is still a tip?' Miranda tried to sound more good-humoured than she felt.

'Only in the eye of potential tenants. You may not believe how picky they've got.' The agent, who'd given her a lift from Pulborough train station, was friendly enough in a straight-talking way. She wore a stone-coloured linen suit, and sensible shoes for walking over miles of indoor surfaces. 'In here, for example, you might care to change the sofa – I can see it was once rather good of its kind – and maybe do without those curtains altogether. That is, if no one here minds people being able to see in after dark.'

Miranda said nothing; over recent weeks she'd known nothing would make her sleep here on her own. Ideally, anywhere without the paraphernalia of a full-on siege: peepholes, deadlocks, panic buttons. Thank God Richard was on his way down to join her for the weekend, starting with dinner in the village at the Royal Oak.

'If your aunt doesn't want to redecorate, maybe you could find some pictures to go over the, um, more irregular bits.'

So after the agent had checked her watch and shaken hands in farewell – 'Don't be disheartened. It won't seem so bad, afterwards' – Miranda started checking what pictures were left. After an hour of staggering about with paintings almost too wide to lift, she'd had it. Besides she wanted clear of here while it was still light. Before leaving she went to check that nothing important had been left in the barn.

Then outside the back door… She even spoke the words out loud: Of *course*.

Another pig-mask, its down-turned eyes and mouth elegantly grotesque. But this one was familiar, almost to invisibility. She even remembered the words painted on the inside: Sad Pig. For all of two years it had been here on the farmhouse wall, now half smothered by a climbing hydrangea.

It had been designed as one of a pair, fired and decorated here in Kitty's studio. But by whom? She called Kitty.

'Well, no, they weren't by me,' her aunt told her. 'I remember Josh saying he ought to call it a collaboration. Between the two of us, I mean. But no, it really is all his own... I hope one day you can give both those masks a good home. Sometimes it's easier to be sentimental about other people's work, at least if you knew them well or saw them doing it. So often with your own all you remember is what a damned great effort it took.'

Miranda hoped her aunt still had at least one commission in hand and said as much. She preferred not to think of Kitty as no longer working.

'I should say so! Besides, it'll give me an excuse to avoid various people in here. I've nothing against other old women as such; it's just that you want a change from them sometimes.'

She added, 'In a way now, I'm glad I was interned, all those years ago. It was frightfully squalid, of course. But you never know, especially later in life, when the experience of having been confined might be useful. And, my God, you did meet all sorts.' Kitty, in France as a language student, had been put in a camp with other aliens and so-called enemy women. To Miranda and Josh it had always been a disappointment that she was so unforthcoming with her memories. 'And afterwards?' they'd once demanded. 'Tell us about the escape.' All they'd known was that she'd got home many months later via Spain. 'I don't think so,' she'd told them. 'It was all too dreary. I shouldn't even have bothered to make the effort.'

Now, not knowing if her aunt was about to confide for once, Miranda said, 'If you'd stayed in the camp would you have got home just as soon?'

'Who knows? Either way it would have been a time of stupendous dullness. All that queuing, for every imaginable thing.' To show the subject closed after all, she added, 'Look, about the stuff I've left unsorted ... yes, well specifically the paperwork ... I'm sorry it's such an avalanche of crap; I'll help with it when I'm mobile again. In the meantime, if you can bear it, with all the other stuff you'd better just have a free hand.'

*

The difference a few days can make. That weekend they were bivouacking in the empty farmhouse after Richard had said he wanted to see more of Stumblehurst, as a place from Miranda's childhood.

Sunday morning, first thing.

'And now good morrow to our waking souls.' Propped on one elbow, he was looking at her. His speech was faintly slurred from sleep.

Miranda had been bathed in gratitude at rising towards consciousness to find them here like this. But only for a splinter of time. They would have made a pretty sight, she thought. So long as you didn't know better. Now that they were probably about to split.

At first she hadn't thought of them as lovers; just two people who saw themselves as adults doing what came naturally. Knowing they might never meet again, it had seemed the simplest way to thank him for every recent act of friendship. To show by deed, not words, how much she wished him well.

The perfect parting gift, she'd told herself – one that pleasured both of them to the limit. It wasn't as if she'd want to remember him with regret, at having denied him. There weren't that many men you could like so unreservedly. But now. She really hadn't thought to lead him on; in fact she'd never meant either of them to be lured this far.

As for being serenaded with verse, John Donne was too bruisingly upbeat by far, now that Richard's departure might be only weeks away. On the other hand it seemed a bit late to draw back from a harmless bit of quote and counter-quote.

'Thou sun art half as happy as we,

In that the world's contracted thus.'

She too sounded half drowned by torpor. Sometimes sleep was the most euphoric drug of all. What was great about it wasn't just the alertness, the impatience for another day, that comes from eight hours straight, but that first langorous rising to consciousness through fathoms of snooze.

'That bit's not right.'

'Yes, it is.'

'It's not even the same poem.'

'I got the poet though. And even if it's not the same poem, it's the right one.'

Richard flopped back onto his pillow and gazed into the skeletal grooves and ridges of a ceiling beam. The timbers of this house, Kitty said, had once been part of a warship. It was hard to see how; they seemed too crooked to have come from anything that had floated, much less bumped about on an open sea.

He said, 'A room like this certainly needs to be the whole world. To make up for sleeping on these godawful cushions.' They were making do on a bare upstairs floor. It was late; the sun had risen clear of the Beacon and was striking straight down through the uncurtained window.

'Was this your room?' For the last few days they'd been mapping each other's previous life, like a couple of kids scampering about exploring at the start of a holiday.

'It doesn't feel that way now. Unless I concentrate hard, on something like the view. Or up at that ceiling.' Rags of cobweb were draped from the beams, now as always clotted with dust. In its ghostly state, the room combined transience and enduring memory like pieces of film imposed one on the other. Once, because here Miranda had been a child, at play and self-absorbed, it had been a centre of the universe. She said as much.

There was a pause before Richard responded. 'Just like now.'

Another beat of silence as if, like a bungled trapeze routine, the next thought might miss its chance of being spoken. He added, 'Only we're practising at grown-up stuff as well.'

It was almost the voice of uncomplicated pleasure, aware of nothing but itself. But there was something else: some small doubt or fear, no bigger than a draught needling its way through a keyhole into a warm room.

'I don't feel like a grown-up,' Miranda said. 'More like a kid who's nicked the icing off someone else's cake.'

'Are you thinking the same as me? I mean, seriously?'

She tensed all over – she couldn't help it. 'Is this something I want to hear?' 'Serious' wasn't always something you could say, much less be, when naked in one another's arms. Each of them pulled away. Wary, but pretending not to be.

Richard looked at her. He was trying to respond as a man, but the very effort made him seem younger, like the engaging idiot he used to be.

Wanting to make things easy for him, she started to say something bantering. But he ignored her.

'America,' he said. 'Come with me.' It didn't sound like a request; just a flat statement of desire. His determination not to plead was absolute.

She couldn't agree to what he wanted – she knew that, before he'd finished speaking. But for several moments she still didn't know what to say.

That made it worse; right away he'd fooled himself into thinking she couldn't decide. He was already halfway to shining with delight as he said, 'I've always wanted to say that to you!'

'Always?' she said lamely.

'For days – what's the difference?'

'I hope you're not one of those guys who think they've got to tie some kind of knot with every woman who beds them. If that's how you are, I've been warned about men like you.'

'Miranda, in God's name!' He fell back against his pillow and stared unseeing at the ceiling.

'I'm sorry,' she said, prone beside him. They didn't dare touch each other. 'I'm sorry. I didn't mean to say anything so wrong.'

At that moment neither wanted to hear or speak another word. But all the obvious things had to be said

– right away, while they still lay like a couple of effigies under their hastily pulled-up sheet. So Miranda did that, reciting the facts like a teacher half expecting to be ignored by the whole class. Since Adam's marriage she'd had nearly no money; without money she couldn't study in the States. So how could she go with him, and still join the profession which now and always was her life's great love?

Through everything she said, he neither moved nor spoke. Later they took it in turns to get up, without either saying a word. On the drive back, at first they were careful only to talk about unimportant things. It didn't seem they'd properly left the farmhouse while they were still threading their way through deep lanes and overhanging woods. But coming to the main road and the first signboards to London, one of them, then the other, gave an involuntary sigh: a return to the world of striving and serious concerns. Several miles on, past the first motorway intersection with its rear-view panorama of heathland and downs, Richard asked her out to dinner. 'To make the most of the time we've still got.'

She glanced at him while he concentrated on overtaking a line of cars, but saw no lingering hostility or anger.

'Yes, let's do that,' she said – though she didn't really believe he'd given up on luring her away to a life of – what? – temporary secretarial work? – in New Jersey. She should have felt at least a prickle of guilt, at not planning a clean break the moment they got to London. Instead she added, 'I'd love to.'

Thirty

TRAGIC FANNY HAD IT COMING

That was what one former pal of Frances 'Hot Fanny' Brooke confided to our reporter following the high-class hooker's bizarre death.

'How could I know how really insecure she was? I mean, we just had a lot of fun,' said Peter, one-time love-romp companion to kinky Frances, 22. Modestly he prefers not to give his full name.

'I'm not saying we didn't enjoy doing things that other people would find a bit, well, saucy. But that's exactly why no one would expect her to finish it all in the amazing way she did.'

So just how did the posh pro with the off-the-scale 'Phwoarr' rating meet her TRULY ODDBALL end?

Said downcast ex-Romeo Peter: 'She seemed so carefree. I mean, she was really something.' He looked rueful as he added, 'Together we did things you might not believe. And now this.'

THIS was the fancy-dress farewell to life of an exotic lovely who decided to die as she had lived – OUTRAGEOUSLY.

THIS was the end-it-all snub aimed at her wacky high-

rolling life by a lusty lass who found in the end that she DIDN'T have it all. Who was doomed to discover that a glittering career as one of London's most expensive call-girls couldn't compensate for her secret inner emptiness.

And THIS was how she arranged for her body to be found. 'You couldn't make it up,' Peter told us, with a sad shake of his head. 'She was wearing...'

There was a photo of course. The caption read: 'The raunchy reveller who staged orgies yet died tragically'. As well as Frances, the picture included several other people in their year at St Edmund's. Most available snaps would have showed Frances looking up with a diffident smile; against the odds they'd found one where she was laughing out loud.

Miranda recognized it: taken in a local pub during Rag Week. Everyone wore whatever bits of dressing-up-box idiocy they'd been able to find. Frances was wrapped in a large – and, Miranda recalled, very dusty – black ostrich-feather boa with antique tassels. Also grinning straight to camera, Miranda wore a body-stocking under a junk-shop flapper dress shredded by age and the weight of its own beading. Above her head a male hand, maybe Thomas's, made a show of brandishing a lidded two-pint stein of beer. A shadowy profile in the background was Richard, identifiable by a bushranger's hat from which he'd hung a dozen champagne corks.

Standing in the busy street, Miranda cursed aloud and flung the paper away. Its pages fanned out and tore, and one or two passers-by gave her sharp a look. She had to humiliate herself by picking it all up and swore again as she stuffed it in a litter bin.

She'd bought most of that day's papers. In the tunnel near Gloucester Road station there was a signal check, so Miranda had time to read almost everything about Frances. The longest article quoted several sources, all seemingly from the police. There was Leese; and a couple of inches were given to a Detective Constable described as a friend of the family. Both seemed anxious not to say anything that sounded like their own opinion, and no one mentioned that Frances had been a sex worker. 'My colleagues and I entirely respect the ruling of the coroner,' Leese had said. 'In our view an open verdict is the only acceptable one in a tragic case like this.'

If Wragg suspected differently he wasn't saying so. 'Yes,' he'd responded, 'I have heard it alleged that Miss Brooke, for whatever reason, had been seeking treatment for a mild case of depression. More than that, however, I am not empowered to say.'

There'd been no comment from either of Frances' parents. So that was that.

*

At least it was a comfort to see some of what was done for her. The funeral was in the chapel at St Edmund's, a stately Baroque building in the courtyard of the Old Hospital. Two chunky nude statues reclined opposite each other over the main doorway, representing Sickness and Health. The last time Miranda had been in here, it was at a service for the elderly stranger whose cadaver she'd recently finished cutting up. Afterwards she'd felt a fraud, being thanked for attending by a small group of old people who'd known him.

Today a lot of senior hospital staff were there, including the Dean himself, sitting just behind the front pews reserved for next of kin. On one side of the main aisle was Phil, accompanied by Leese and a couple of people who may also have been policemen. DC Rosa Hill was with them, semi-anonymous in a basic-black trouser suit and neat tied-back hair. The opposite side of the front row – the one, Miranda realized, where at a wedding the bride's family sat – was occupied only by a couple of women in their forties. One, whom Miranda figured for Frances' mother, was sharply dressed, with brightly coloured hair, classically 'good' accessories and long slender legs. The other had a family likeness, only in a matronly version with every colour and shape softened or blurred. An elder sister of the mother, perhaps. Against a discreet background of organ music and in front of a coffin heaped with flowers, no one gave any sign of what they thought or felt.

She hadn't known that Frances had had so few near relatives. They were easily outnumbered by the students there, scattered a few rows back from where the Dean and the Chancellor sat with their wives, all in dark suits. A hundred years ago most people of twenty or so, with large families and shorter life expectancy, must have known in detail what to wear to a funeral. Here most had taken a chance and dressed as for a lecture, only in sober colours: leather jackets, black denims, some specially ironed white shirts. Thomas stood out in a well-cut three-piece. Somehow Miranda had known he'd show respect by dressing formally. Richard too was wearing a suit, though it made him look so unfamiliar that she nearly did a double-take, sliding into the seat he'd indicated next to him.

The hospital choral society was there too, all robed up. After some formal words of greeting from the Chaplain they rose to their feet amid a vivid silence and gave forth the opening bars of a Bach anthem: terse, dignified music declaring unutterable reassurance. Tears swelled in Miranda's eyes and her hands were suddenly busy with nothing. Already there was a gale of nose-blowing throughout the congregation. For Frances herself, or as a response to any early death?

At least this congregation saw some form of death most working days. Not one so ignorant of tragedy that they could now stoop to luxuriate in melancholy or be enlivened by horror.

Except that... like a sleepwalker shaken by waking in an unfamiliar place, Miranda was confronted with the thought she feared the most.

Is *he* here?

If Frances didn't die by choice or accident, he'd have to be present. Miranda knew that if she herself been in that coffin beneath its mass of cream-coloured roses and white chrysanthemums nothing could have kept him away. And he wouldn't be skulking in the gallery, where no one below could glimpse him without turning round to stare.

At such a moment the person who'd written and texted her those vile messages would never have settled for anything but sitting down here in plain view.

Or could her friend's case have nothing to do with her own after all? Had Frances' 'he' been a 'she'? A jealous wife? Or an unlikely client, full of years and public respect. Miranda knew she could go mad, looking at everyone here in turn, from the weather-beaten Chaplain, a former missionary whose self-taught knowledge of East African tribal music was said to be unequalled, to the youngest woman chorister, whose tongue stud glinted every time she opened her mouth.

Maybe there was just no such person.

Nothing in the service even hinted at an unnatural death, let alone violence. The one acknowledged purpose for being there was to offer the survivors some comfort – if that's how you'd describe so much mention of a brilliant career cut short. From the pulpit the Dean praised Frances as having 'the potential for medical inquiry at its finest, in her persistent, unassuming quest for excellence'. And Jeanette gave a reading in the least actressy voice imaginable: one that put the words into your mind as though she weren't there and you'd just thought of them yourself.

'...And God shall wipe away all tears from their eyes; and there shall be no more death, neither sorrow, nor crying, neither shall there be any more pain: for the former things are passed away...'

Of all the people there, Jeanette was the only one to hint at the squalor of Frances' death. 'We all know what we've been told to think of her, these last few days,' she said, on standing in the pulpit to give her reading. 'But in the real world this is how we, her friends and allies, remember and cherish her.'

Only the presence of so many off-duty police was a reminder that no one had merely fallen asleep in the embrace of the angels. Individually they didn't seem like a casting director's idea of how coppers should be; as a group they looked unmistakable. One of them, Detective Sergeant Wragg, whose name Miranda recognized from that morning's papers, stood up to give the final address. He looked bland and roly-poly, and spoke with touching restraint of his friendship with the family and his memories of Frances as a little girl. Then it was time for everyone to stand up and restore themselves with a full-throated rendering of 'For All the Saints' before going out into the sunlight.

The congregation trickled across the main courtyard, feeling obliged even in the open to keep their voices down. Inside the oldest of the lecture rooms, all dark wood panelling, a buffet lunch had been laid out down the centre of the room. There was an immediate change, like a movie whose characters fade up as their confident later self. People crowded along the table where drinks were served and the noise of talk increased.

Several weddings Miranda had gone to were like this once the awful-solemnities bit was over. As in the chapel the room soon divided between unconnected tribes. The students, uncertain how to behave, formed little groups of their own. Most of the older hospital staff and their spouses seemed to be networking just as at any departmental party. One of the waiters had paused to laugh about something with Richard, and Thomas had been buttonholed by Mr Jameson, beside whom he looked less like a mature student than a fast-rising colleague already cushioned by a secure salary. A few people made the effort to cross one of the room's invisible lines: Frances' mother and the seeming relative with her were being tended in particular by the courteous Professor of Anatomy and his wife.

It was impossible to guess what either of the two women thought or felt. But some funerals could be like that – couldn't they? The stoic bereaved parent, valiant beyond belief, who then dropped dead the week after.

But not in this case, something murmured from the back of her mind. Only twice had Miranda heard Frances mention her mother. The second time, she recalled, was when they were sitting outside the mews pub on the evening before Miranda left their flat-share. A becalmed occasion with not much said, as if one of them was about to make a journey. What on earth, though, had brought forth the subject of death? Whatever it was, Frances had seemed to stare at some distant thing beyond any physical line of sight as she'd said, 'When I die, I wouldn't mind leaving a message.'

How unsuspecting she'd been. 'Me too,' she'd replied. 'Maybe in deeds, though; not words.'

'I like to think I'd leave a message for my mother. With her name on it and everything.' Frances spoke in an almost-murmur, as unexcited as if making a shopping list. Miranda turned in vain to hear what words she might have in mind. But when her friend spoke next it was of something or other quite different.

Had anyone else heard her talk like that? If so, no

wonder an unspoken verdict of suicide now loured over the whole gathering.

Throughout, Frances' parents weren't even pretending to notice each other. Phil stayed near the bar amid his clannish mates. Apart from Leese, who drank up and left before anyone else, they were soon the least subdued people in the room. Queuing plate in hand by the heaps of smoked salmon and chicken salad, Miranda found it impossible not to overhear.

'A great girl.' Phil sounded reflective but not particularly sad. He seemed like a man who'd expected to feel a lot worse. From the look of him he'd already downed several units on the way there. Had this been an occasion where a photographer roamed about snapping everyone his face would have printed up shiny as chrome.

What reasons had he for turning up half drunk? Bravado in the face of his unreconciled ex-wife? Shock and anger, at having his dead daughter paraded by the gutter press like the carcass of a defeated enemy? A survivor's self-blame, grieving for someone who shouldn't have died?

Or, mixed with all this brew of passions, was there relief at knowing that after today the publicity would mercifully dwindle away? No one now would shout or murmur, Foul play! The coroner's charitable report had seen to that.

'She was too,' one of the men with him was saying. 'Truly a great girl.' A taut silence followed, which Miranda took at first for embarrassment on Phil's behalf.

But no one looked uncomfortable and two of them swapped a quick glance with him that seemed to say, I'm easy with this if you are. On the edge of the group Rosa

Hill emptied her nearly full glass and briskly turned away to order another orange juice. Phil insisted, 'I don't care how often I say this. Because it deserves to be said. She was all heart. She was. All heart. A real trier. True grit, that's what that girl had.'

'A woman of parts,' added Wragg. Back down from the pulpit, his public-address manner cast off, he too looked as if he'd stopped off on the way for a few sharpeners. There was another silence, as though each remark was being tested by the group to see if it was all right to carry straight on.

'And every one of them working.' This from the youngest man there, a tall pale guy who looked more like most people's idea of a trainee clergyman. He couldn't resist glancing around, almost as if hoping someone would laugh. No one looked up. Wragg laid a hand on his shoulder, and this time there was no hesitation as the older man said, 'A splendid woman in every way. I'm proud to raise my glass to her.'

'Too right.'

'She'll be missed.'

'In every way. Just like you say, Phil.'

'You did us a great honour, Phil. Helping us to make her acquaintance.'

Phil waved his glass in a saddened gesture of magnanimity. No doubt he meant it. Maybe each of them had set out that day wanting to show respect. But something else glinted through. Once you noticed it, you saw it in each of them. The pale young guy's guilty tremor of excitement. Wragg's reined-in wariness. Leese's face closing down like a steel shutter. Miranda left her half-filled plate and stepped up to them.

She couldn't help it. Not once they'd failed to hide their aura of smug conspiracy. She'd no idea what she was going to say. Nor had she stopped to wonder what their part had been in Frances' months of whoring – what kind of knowledge or complicity. But suddenly there she was: about to lose it in public yet also an inquisitive witness at the spectacle of her own rage.

Only Phil turned around. The others looked into their drinks, rigid as a game of statues. It was impossible to pay more attention than they gave Miranda at that moment.

She said, 'I'm glad to know Frances was appreciated so well.'

Her other self took in Thomas and Richard, threading their way over as a matter of urgency. The same part of her, the onlooker, thought, Do I actually look this angry? followed by, Will they get here before whatever I say next?

She added, 'By all of you especially, I mean.'

She'd been wrong if she'd expected an abrasive put-down. As a group they just evaporated into the crowd, prompt as some special effect. At the same moment, Thomas touched her on the elbow with a prompt murmur of 'Miranda – let me get you something to eat.'

'Are you all right?' Richard asked as soon as she'd nodded at Thomas, dumb with gratitude at their intrusion.

'Oh, yes!' she finally managed. Her voice came out breathy and half an octave sharp. 'I'm totally fine!' Immediately she added, 'I'm sorry. I don't mean that. It's a fib.'

Another step backward in the quest to become a grown-up. *Stop*, she told herself. Don't start using this man all over again, only this time as a confidant. God, how she wanted to tell him every single thing she felt right then. But no: she was practising. For when he was gone. Anything else would have been dishonest.

Thirty-one

'All In It Together' read the opening caption. On Miranda's VDU there'd come into view the first of Frances' files that she'd so hastily pirated.

A film of three naked people in wigs and masks. At first glance they were just standing wedged together like an improbable set of conjoined triplets. Then the men, one in front of the woman, one behind, began carefully to move against her, each in turn.

She realized she'd never seen Frances unclothed before. Her long narrow hands and feet were mainly what identified her.

Was *he* here? The man who may have killed Frances and who – if indeed he was the same – seemed to convince the police that his stalking Miranda was just a jape. The two men on-screen, now posting their way from the equivalent of a trot to a canter, could have been anyone. She ran the film faster – then slowed it again. How squeamish, to see poor Frances speeded up at her work and twitching like a marionette in some cinematic farce.

But what a lot of it there was. In the end she accelerated the images regardless, pausing only when a new file brought a change of partners. Some group scenes included other women – if not sex workers, maybe civilians out to test their mettle for a dare. Some people played up so grossly to the camera and in such tight close-up, it was hard to see what they were flaunting; you might as well be watching a fibre-optic traverse someone's gut. The quality varied. Some images were sharp enough to be professional; other sequences were all false colours and random highlights, so that you'd be pushed to recognize your own self. One trio, backed by a bad recording of classical sitar music, was so home-movie that the shadows on each naked body were mossy green.

All the more frustrating when something here finally snagged her memory. How, though? What was it about one trio, once more wearing only masks and joke wigs

Frances again. And a woman in a cat mask and a straight black wig, its colour at odds with her light pubic hair. Her taste, or maybe the preference of the man, ran to passive, rag-doll sex, though twice she spoiled the effect of unfettered passion by leaning towards a bedside table for a surreptitious snort.

The standard of headgear varied. In contrast with the other woman's Amateurs Night kit, over the top half of her face Frances wore a beautiful feathered mask, like something copied from an anthropological museum. The man with her, seen at first from behind, looked like he'd sold their game short and just settled for pulling a stocking over his head. But then he turned around to face the camera.

Now this she had seen before.

His mask. An elaborate pig-face featuring a half-human smile and vivid curlicues like a Maori tattoo. In itself it was simply a handsome piece of work. So why, among all these other self-conscious couplings, did this detail cause a blip of unease?

Then into her memory a time and place flipped up. For God's sake: the studio at Stumblehurst. She was there when this was being made. It was the partner – she forgot the name – of Sad Pig, now taken home for safekeeping.

With this realization came a dismal ache of possibility. If this was Josh's creation…? Please don't let one of these people be him.

Immediately she chided herself for an idiot. No one here had her brother's tall narrow body, a boy's angularity only now filling out to make a grown man. The guy in the pig mask was no more than average height; plus he obviously worked out.

Apart from Frances surely no one here could have been identified while merely tangled round each other in ways they fancied unusual. At least one of them could be seen saying something; but the feeble soundtrack only came out as the nonsense words in your head at the instant of falling asleep. If only they'd take a break on camera, to do normal stuff like drink a cup of tea or yawn. If *he* was here, who knew if he mightn't be recognizable? By his walk perhaps, or the way he held a cigarette.

An extraordinary range of male bodies was offered for inspection. Some were beautiful, in a way that many men take for granted in their twenties. Others were old enough for their body hair to have turned almost white. A lot of middle-aged nakedness saw itself as bold and free – except that no one went far enough to show their face.

There could be several reasons for this coy anonymity. Knowing how this really made you look, perhaps; a couple of older women were like saggy cavorting sofas. Any of them might have wanted not to compromise their marriage or their standing in the world. And no way was it hard to list the usual-suspect professions that got serviced by someone like Frances. Doctor; politician; judge…

Policeman.

Frances' funeral. The horrible little scene between those four coppers. At the time she'd let the full truth of it slide past her. From squeamishness, but also wanting to be unsuspicious and nice: yes, well maybe they knew how Frances earned her keep….

But knowledge of the carnal sort? Complicity in whoring her? She saw it now without a doubt. Every man of them had had her. With her stepfather more than ready to lead the way. That could be him right there on screen, frozen in the final frame and lying back like an exhausted gladiator.

How could she have missed something so obvious? Thrilled with what must have started as a private relationship, and pleased with Frances and with himself, maybe he couldn't have helped showing off, to the point of passing her round his ex-colleagues. Especially since – Frances had said – he'd been hard up.

She felt at first an unreasoned queasy complicity in everything, coy or gross, that she was witnessing. By the end of the evening she was past knowing what evidence mattered, let alone who or what she should dread. At midnight she went into the bedroom, took off her shoes and lay down on the bed, too tired to wash or undress even though her clothes made her hot. At last she fell asleep, aching all over.

Thirty-two

In seeking Josh she was waiting for one particular day. It came and Miranda left her flat early. The day was bright and busy; radios blared through open car windows and the crowds on the Gloucester Road were as sunburned and sweat-stained as if they lived like this the year round. High summer, prematurely autumnal, was brassy and climate-changed with plane trees in the nearby square already losing their leaves.

Some people on the Tube were still half asleep, commuters roosting where they stood and tuning out a party of over-excited foreign schoolgirls who might have been Korean. In the sweltering carriage some lives were hard to picture: one woman cradled a newborn asleep within a snowy splash of broderie anglaise. Her beefy arms and shoulders were so densely tattooed, they made her look blue with cold.

Five stops on in a tree-filled Edwardian suburb it was like having a blindfold taken off in another country. Miranda sought a mansion block on a bend of the river, with a half-mile view in each direction. The tide was out and acres of mud lay silvered in the sun. Traces of early-morning steam rose from the central channel, where the day's first tour boats for Hampton Court slowly jockeyed in each other's wake.

Having phoned at a shameless hour she'd got lucky. Ollie should actually be there today, back from a trip with friends cruising off the Dalmatian coast. The phone had been answered by his grandmother. 'Oh, but I don't think he'll want to be disturbed before at least ten o'clock.' Undeterred, Miranda was now pressing the big doorbell in its circular brass surround, confident that poor Ollie wouldn't have the heart to hold out on her.

And so it proved. His hot-faced unease at thwarting her was now paramount as she faced him down. '…For God's sake, Ollie! I bet you only promised not to tell me about living on the boat…'

By ten o'clock she was already on the other side of town, juddering through Hackney on a crowded bus. Among the other passengers, so far three impatient mothers had each addressed her complaining small child in a different language.

The address Ollie had given lay on a main road of small Turkish shops and bleak cafés with a client base of elderly Cypriot men. Miranda felt queasy with hope. Fearful, too. If she was about to find Josh, would he yet forgive her?

The place she'd been looking for was a squat. It was housed in a newish but disused warehouse which must have been built on the site of a handsome Queen Anne mansion; some elegant railings and a tall wrought-iron gate were still there. Approaching it someone strode past her and disappeared round a corner of the warehouse. He wore a top hat with a leopard-skin hatband into which was tucked a preserved rosebud dyed green. Overall his kit was a stylish mixture of Alice in Wonderland with old-time aviator. Like most urban tribal costumes it made Miranda feel she never took enough trouble with how she herself looked.

At first the empty warehouse seemed deserted. Its entrance was up an alley and through a pair of sliding metal doors. They were almost closed and too heavy to move; it was a squeeze to get through. Inside, she could guess why this place lay closed to the world. This wasn't a household but a village. A lost settlement, wary of being found. Every home was some kind of motor, so it was like finding yourself shrunk down to the same scale as a collection of antique Dinky models, with toy people living in each vehicle. There were a couple of buses with curtains at the windows: one an old double-decker Routemaster, the other looking like Thomas the Tank Engine's friend Bertie. Nearby was an ancient ambulance from the fifties, the sort you saw in Ealing comedies. Only one home, a camper van, looked less than twenty years old. Washing was hung out on lines and there was even a playground of sorts, with a swing and an improvised seesaw. It wouldn't have been out of place to see chickens scratching about.

'Are you from the Independent?'

She was being questioned by a woman who'd just manhandled a Calor gas container out onto the top of a horsebox ramp. All sorts of stuff was stacked inside, like in an old-time general store. The woman was solidly built, with a round, attentive face. But anyone expecting to see a hippie earth mother would have been dead wrong. She wore a straight black knee-length skirt, black pumps and a clean white cotton shirt. Her hair was strained back in a ponytail. She reminded Miranda of a theatre nurse she knew at St Edmund's.

No, she said, she wasn't from any part of the press and offered to help with the gas container.

'No, let's leave it. I'm late for work anyway. Only, someone's got to be here to do an interview later on.' The woman opened the cab door of the horsebox from outside and stood on the step beneath it to reach inside for a jacket. It matched her skirt, and once she put it on, she'd become the very type of a neat young office worker. Anonymous but sharpish, in a way that could either mean an invisible receptionist, pleasant to people who weren't always polite back, or a rising recruit, rigorously picked, her prospects too serious for clothes that got noticed.

What was the interview about? Miranda asked, after explaining why she was there.

'Oh, the working homeless, I think. Or was it just a magazine article about this part of town? ... And yes, of course I remember Joshie Faulds.'

'Remember? He is alright, isn't he?'

'Fine, the last I heard. Only he ran out of money to put in the pot. He said something about staying with friends. Once they're back in London.'

Till then?

'The Fairmead Estate, I think he said. I've got an A-Z—'

'Near Albany Square?' Miranda recalled Laura describing the place. Back then GPs were more likely to make house calls and the estate had been nearly new instead of semi-derelict.

The woman said, 'I'm afraid he didn't leave any flat number. People don't, do they, when they think it's somewhere they'll only be for a few days.'

Miranda understood the distinction she was making. As squats went, this one seemed fairly settled. There were even ornaments in the windows of several vehicles, and a circle of scruffy folding chairs was ranged around a recently used barbecue. The woman saw her looking around and said, 'It's a shame he couldn't stay. This is better than a lot of places. Even if you haven't got an office or something as well. You know, where you can always shower first thing and then finish getting dressed.'

As Miranda was leaving, the woman said, 'He – Joshie – he isn't in trouble? I mean, you don't work for someone, do you?'

'It's just family stuff – but could he be in trouble?'

'I don't think so. He wasn't – I mean, isn't – the type, is he?' But a look of doubt shaded her face. She hesitated, then said, 'I know it's none of my business. But what he said was, he'd got no family.'

*

The tower blocks of the Fairmead Estate were already visible from outside the squat, like dirty thumb-marks on the city's nearest horizon. They stood at the end of a straight busy road, the sort whose name alters every half mile or so. It was also a townscape where buildings kept changing their identity. The Temperance Hall on the corner of the local High Road had long since become a mosque, with added starveling minarets and a token dome. The former stables at the one-time tram depot housed a Chinese youth club where visiting royals came to see dragon dances performed. And a dire block of flats, like a foundered prison ship, had replaced the hunting box among whose walks and arbours Samuel Pepys had seen his first orange tree.

First the prim, rule-bound world of Pickerel's Ait; then the not quite legal good order of the communal squat in the warehouse. Boscastle House, which was Josh's address on the estate, marked another downward step. It rose above a scuffed area of grass by a nineteen-sixties parade of shops starved nearly to death for lack of custom. A betting shop had survived; also a glum café where even the strip lighting was greasy, plus a funeral parlour whose window held an urn and a bunch of plastic flowers. The entrance to the tower block was through a pair of glass doors under a decomposing concrete canopy. One door had a large star-shaped fracture. It was hard to believe this building looked down from only a quarter mile on the island of trees that held Miranda's old home in Albany Square.

Rather than look for Josh right away, she found she preferred to go into the café. In its window she sat down by a dying spider plant, with a coffee served in a thick white cup, the kind that hospital caterers use.

She almost missed Josh when he came out. Mainly because of the change in how he looked.

Lost. As in done away with; missing in action; gone. In

another time, another place, some new things about him would count for nothing. The ratty hair and half-grown beard would be fine on someone who'd just done a week's survival course. And his clothes were still only rumpled, not sagging in tatters.

What made him hard to recognize was the boy within. Miranda recognized the clothes he wore; they were partly how she'd noticed him. Only, now he seemed to have shrunk. The way he slouched along as if defying his own lack of purpose. His absent, preoccupied look, where bewilderment lurked. No longer was there any glimpse in him of future manhood. He walked across the road towards the café, not seeing her, then turned and went up the street.

Nothing could save you from pity like this. Drowning in sadness, she hastened to follow him. Wherever he was bound.

Thirty-three

It was like an alternative reality, one where we'd lost World War II. The sleek harshness of Canada Wharf was more so on days when its windswept spaces were almost empty. It became a disused stage set where straggles of tourists came to stare upwards and look lost. Even the river, at this point really an arm of the North Sea, looked small: a distant twinkling prospect. Below a narrow, fast-moving sky the great towers were giants striding in file.

But any day of the week featured the purposeful business-suited figures you'd imagine in the architects' drawings. No wonder Josh stood out in this pitiless, kempt place. Against the pleached limes and yew hedges of Canada Square Miranda's brother looked like a piece of sentient litter. She watched from a distance as he stationed himself by the main entrance leading to Adam's office. So that's why he was here. As a magazine seller, accosting people on their way out to lunch.

Close to, anyone could see he wasn't trading for real. He had no seller's registration badge and only one copy of the magazine to hold out at an unresponsive scurrying public. It wasn't even up to date; Miranda recognized the same edition of the Big Issue that she'd left for him on the boat.

Just as she was braced to go towards him, he raised his voice. From a defeatist mumble he'd switched to shouting his wares like a barking dog. He was scuttling sideways alongside three expensively dressed men with briefcases who strode towards the main entrance of Canada Tower. With each shout he got more insistent.

'Big Issue! Big *Issue!* *Big Issue!*' It was a demand, all right. But not for anything as ordinary as a pound coin for one superannuated copy and have a nice day.

One of the men glanced at him in passing as he and his companions reached the top of the steps and vanished inside the building. That's odd, Miranda thought. If you're pretending someone's not there, as these men were with Josh, you'd never risk catching their eye.

Then, with a lurch of dismay she understood the man's involuntary glance and quickened pace.

That person walking by had been their father.

What Adam had seen at first wasn't Josh, but some anonymous street person: one identity fits all. Only then had his self-possession been shaken, by the revelation that this was his son lurking hopelessly in the windy space beneath his office. Miranda watched as Adam strode out of sight, into his world of well-judged words shared behind boardroom doors.

So that's why Josh was here. And why he was squatting in that derelict block with its view down onto his father's house. Josh was seeking to turn his entire outraged life into an accusation.

She couldn't not go up to him, standing amid the lunchtime passers-by. He was staring at nothing, his face tight with the effort of self-containment.

But at that moment a young guy in motorbike messenger kit ran down the steps while looking only at the ground, and accidentally bumped into him, so hard that Josh was spun round.

'Sorry, mate.'

Josh turned to look at him with futile bloody mayhem in his eyes. But by then the other guy was gone, and what he saw was his sister.

'What, then?' said Josh. 'What? What is it? Go on, what? What? What the fuck do *you* want?'

'Joshie—'

He came towards her as if to return a physical blow. 'Yes? Yes, what? *Yes?*'

'If you want, I'll go away. Until some other time.'

'Do that.'

'I need to talk to you.'

'Piss off.'

'For God's sake! I don't mean right now.'

'Thank God for that. Now, go on' – with a dismissive jerk of his head – 'bugger off.'

She took a step towards him. Josh countered with a look that said, I dare you. In a deliberate voice worse than any violence, he told her, 'See it like this. There's nothing – there's nothing at all – that I'd want less than hearing from you.' And turned, and strode away.

Thirty-four

The noises elsewhere in the house were like the pulsing of organs in a healthy body. Adam was in the shower when Miranda arrived that evening. Waiting for him in the drawing room she listened to the routines of a full, busy household. She was forgetting how it felt to live in a home like this. A place where every sound, however small or incidental, is familiar: the opening of each door or the where and who of every footstep. In the master bathroom, between the whoosh of running water you could hear the urbane voices of Radio Four; probably an arts programme. Upstairs someone was vacuuming: maybe Rob the Swab following up a day in the publishing house spent collating proof corrections and writing blurbs. Outside, someone from the firm that did the garden was switching off an electric mower.

The only recognizable voice was Julie's, from the next room where she was deep in a phone conversation. Amid the other indoor sounds it was hard to make out any words. But just from the long gaps and easy cadences you could tell this call was set to last. A couple of teenage girls couldn't be running up a larger bill. By the time the

You Said She's Where?

shower upstairs was shut off, Miranda figured that in the last few minutes she'd heard more of Julie's voice than over the rest of the short time they'd known each other.

'But here's Mum,' she said, as Etta opened the door and went in to take over the phone. Even if Julie's words hadn't all been audible, from her mother's tone there'd be no doubt who was on the line.

'Thomas! It *is* you! How's my boy?'

Adam appeared, dressed right down after his back-from-work shower. You're looking great, he told Miranda; then poured some drinks and held open the French window for her into the garden. In truth she was tired and shabby – but so what? This time surely he'd be the Dad she'd always counted on through every childhood moment of unhappiness or doubt.

He had to be. Her brief time in the borrowed flat was coming to an end. Now that Gopika's family had completed the drawn-out pageant of her wedding, they were putting it up for sale. An estate agency had started sending potential buyers to look the place over and there'd even been a visit from a film-maker specialising in videos of properties for sale. Keeping the flat perfect had become a kind of rent substitute. Whenever viewers found Miranda in, it was hard to know whether or not she counted as an asset. Did she serve to give the place life, in the same way as new houseplants or discreet music? Or did her presence just embarrass people while they looked in the cupboards and checked to see if the doors and windows opened properly?

And after this address, what next? In describing to Adam where Josh had been living, it was hard not to sound anxious for herself. It would have been a lie, to say she didn't see such places foreshadowing her own future.

To all this Adam listened carefully, staring at the ground and taking occasional sips of mineral water. Miranda figured he must be dieting; certainly he was thinner. He seemed too intent at first to respond, and for the first time in months she dared to think, might he actually help?

'By how much do you consider yourself underfunded?' he eventually said. He looked at her with steady seriousness, as if she were a new business acquaintance proposing a deal.

'Dad, all I know is that I can't see how to get by any more. If you could please, please think of a way for me to do it – a loan, perhaps – I could repay it when I'm qualified and working—'

He put up his hand to interrupt her, evidently thinking hard. 'You say housing is your main expense?'

'One of them.'

'And if you had somewhere to live rent free, then you could still cope? Okay, then tell me how this strikes you. You don't have to say yes; you're not under any obligation. But is there a chance that you might find it acceptable to stay here for a while?' Quickly he added, 'To come home, I mean...'

Could she bear to come back? To this ghost-filled house? With herself changed too, into some kind of non-paying guest?

'I would appreciate it, you know.' He looked intent, as if willing her to say yes while thinking about something else. For the first time since the engagement party he didn't look happy.

What choice did she have? Miranda tried not to sound doubtful as she said, 'Dad, of course I want to think about it. I mean – I'm really grateful to you for offering'

Adam ignored her uncertainty, as if that alone would banish it. 'Fine, lovey. I just want you to know that's fine by me.'

Thirty-five

'FYI' was the only description of one email attachment sent to her next morning.

The opening frames were more or less like the original film made for the estate agency. First an establishing shot of Gopika's flat seen from across the street. The view was cleverly angled so that the building seemed framed in tall greenery. You'd think the it stood in a forest clearing, not just next to a couple of scabby half-grown plane trees. Then a shot of Ronald, the uniformed porter, seated in the foyer.

It was impressive how spacious everything looked when done to somewhere you lived. Inside the flat you wondered why there was so little furniture; surely this sitting room could hold more. A grand piano perhaps, or a dining table with drop leaves.

Miranda guessed what was coming. She'd no idea what to expect in particular, but by now she could picture how malevolent it would be.

'Act 4 a new dimension to urban living,' began the wording across the bottom of the screen. 'You thrilled to Act 3.' There followed a still of the front door to the mews flat, with a foreground glimpse of some scene-of-crime tape.

The camera made its way through the apartment more jerkily now, as if hand-held or worn invisibly. Each caption, as it ran from right to left, was linked to a different shot.

'This superb prestige apartment is beautifully presented ...' A view into the nearly full kitchen bin.

'We can now offer a rare opportunity to view this truly stunning interior...' The bathroom, whose cabinet door was open. The camera lingered in close up, emphasising treatments for physical imperfections like athlete's foot, mouth ulcers and eczema.

'This tastefully presented apartment boasts a wealth of luxurious accoutrements...' Another prospect of the bathroom, this time lingering over the opened pedal bin with its freight of used sanitary towels...

No part of the flat was spared. Afterwards Miranda sat for some time in front of her emptied screen. So this was how he had planned it. For every location – work, home or play – she was to get another threatening message.

It was obvious what she was supposed to feel. But this time she wasn't frightened. Just angry. She didn't know rage could do this: move in uninvited, like some invader too big to fit its host animal.

Well, bugger his Act 5. This time she was going home, to a house with the best that locksmithying could offer, and full of people she knew. Whoever he was, he hadn't meant her to feel a surge of energy like this. He'd been painstaking and inventive as ever; but if he thought he'd been giving her his total attention, he was wrong. This wasn't about her. None of it had been. Everything he'd done had been to do with him. A man to be feared, if that's what he wanted. But from where she saw him, also to be despised. An homunculus.

The other thing she set out to do was go away. Without stopping to think or even feel, that same day she called Richard about joining him however briefly in the States. It wouldn't be a commitment, she told herself. At worst she was just playing for time.

A postscript rounded off the vile online attachment. It was a while before she could face giving it due thought. Flashing up before it could be stopped, there came an image of once-lissom discoloured flesh. Made more horrible by Frances' scrappy costume and its bits of swansdown.

'Which room will it be, Miranda? And what luscious stuff will you be wearing?'

Thirty-six

'Truth and Certainty', read the shout line of the leaflets neatly piled on the hall table in Albany Square. They showed Etta, soon to stand as an MEP, suppressing her natural energy the better to seem infallibly gracious. Her blonde good looks were ageless, her hair its usual bouffant smoothness. However it might be for other politicians, in her own case image and reality had melded to make her the same in her campaign photo as in life.

Tonight she'd persuaded Julie to front a dinner party that had nothing to do with her own career. This would be for Thomas, to help him meet some people useful for him to know.

Julie herself was looking too absent-when-present to do the full hostess thing and queen it at table. Maybe the pregnancy was what made her seem as if this occasion was an exam she expected to fail. Fifteen minutes before the guests were due she wandered irresolutely into the kitchen. Miranda was adding chopped chives to the chilled cream of prawn and cucumber soup; in a hurry, wanting to be free in time to pour the drinks.

Julie loitered for a moment without saying anything. Then asked, 'Is he here yet?'

Who did she mean? It was to be a large party, with twelve at table.

'Adam got back half an hour ago…'

But Julie knew that. 'Oh,' she said, as if to herself.

'I'm sorry?' Miranda glanced up, trying not to let the bits of washed chive clump together on top of the soup.

'It's all right,' Julie said, as if to deny she'd spoken, and drifted back out.

When everyone arrived, coming in together on a gust of shared greetings, Miranda was still in the kitchen. She only met them each when taking round another bottle of champagne, by which time everyone was deep in established conversation.

It was soon evident that every guest, as someone from the medical profession, was there because they'd been a friend of her mother. Nabeela Weerasinghe, now a professor of synaptic pharmacology, had once shared a student lodging with Laura: a lamp-lit house with roll-up bamboo walls in the Solomon Islands. Miranda also recognized Dr Andrei Serafinski from the staff of a famous rival to St Edmund's, who'd originally taken a spectacular demotion to get his family out of Moscow and into what they'd seen as the lotus land of council accommodation in Shoreditch. Mr Jameson was there too, with his daughter and his wife, a paediatrician who'd somehow had three children in as many years while managing to keep her job. The teenage daughter had never been to the house before, and while having her glass refilled she mistook Miranda for a professional caterer. Having found out her mistake it was several minutes before the poor girl stopped blushing.

Everyone was bound to sense the ghost of Laura. As they sat down to eat, it was obvious how much was unchanged. The view into the perfect late-summer garden. The table whose settings looked good enough to eat: all the silver, glassware and damask that Miranda's parents had bought as soon as they could afford dinners like this. Everything in fact, except the change of hosts, along with the tensions they brought to the party on this hot, windless evening. Adam and Julie seemed oblivious of each other, almost like an adulterous couple trying to hide their affair. Julie had little to say and avoided looking directly at anyone.

Knowing what she now did, Miranda couldn't help picturing Julie as she'd been in that sad, sordid video. This was the insubstantial woman who now sat in Laura's place. And yet she could still feel sorry for her. How extraordinary to have two relationships at once with the same person. It was like looking at one of those cheap pendant images that change with the angle at which they're seen. She despised and resented Julie; she also pitied her for having such a mother. Etta herself, trying to lead conversation like a teacher with a discussion group, was behaving as though her son was the only other person in the room. 'Thomas,' she said, as Miranda cleared away the soup plates, 'tell us what you're planning for your year overseas.'

Woman, what have I to do with thee? might have been an apt response. But Thomas, more restrained than Jesus Christ at such a moment, only said, 'Yes, Ma, of course. But right now I'm talking to Elena.' He turned again to Mr Jameson's wife, who'd been listening to each fellow guest with the same steady attentiveness she showed in her consulting room.

'I'm sorry, dear. I didn't mean to interrupt.'

Yet Etta couldn't save herself from nagging her children. 'Oh, good heavens no, Thomas,' she said soon after, when in the kitchen with Miranda he was offering to carry in some plates. 'She can do all that perfectly well on her own. And who shredded the lettuce? This shouldn't have been done yet.'

Miranda had been balancing the beef Wellington on its metal tray while putting it higher in the oven for a final blast of heat. The manoeuvre was tricky, with other dishes to be moved around. In a moment of liberating aggro she lied.

'One of the men did it.'

For all her fierce words of independence, nothing hindered Etta's deference to the opposite sex. Instantly she brightened and softened up.

'Oh... Which one of the men?'

Miranda shut the oven door with a bang, straightened up, and turned to look at her.

'I'll think of someone.'

Overall, dinner wasn't that bad. Most of the guests had been friends for years, and even as strangers they'd have got talking with the ease of professionals who knew each other by reputation. As the sky outside faded to purple and lemony-green, Miranda brought in the branching silver candlesticks Kitty had given Adam and Laura for a wedding present. With the candles lit, each conversation centred on a group of faces seemingly arranged with careful, benevolent purpose.

Even the lack of connection between Adam and Julie wasn't something you had to notice. But Miranda, observing them, didn't know whether to be sad or sceptical. Impossible now, not to picture Laura and Adam together at such parties; saying goodbye to their guests from the front door while fondly wrapped around each other and laughing at God knows what dumb jokes.

Once everyone was gone Adam followed Miranda into the sitting room, where she was clearing up. After she'd moved back home, he'd said, 'You know, Mandy, there's one particular reason why I'm glad you're here. It'll be a good way for you and Julie to get to know each other better. I'm sure she'll be so pleased, if the two of you can spend time together.'

But now he looked urgent and surreptitious, as if he'd been waiting his chance.

'Mandy, you know how one hates people asking for free professional advice. Well, I do, God knows, and I'm sure you'd feel the same.'

Julie had gone to bed, and Etta was rattling about in the kitchen, but he still kept his voice low. 'I just hope you won't think I'm taking advantage.'

'Dad! What is this? Just explain what you want to know, and of course I'll try and tell you.'

'It's nothing, really. You'll simply have to make allowances, lovey, and see it as how some parents-to-be can get, well, just a tad loopy. It happens to fathers too, you know.'

'Well, right. So…?'

His voice dropped to a near-whisper. At least he had the presence of mind not to look behind him.

'Now, this is a matter for complete discretion, you understand—'

'Dad, there's nothing to be ashamed of if you're worried.'

'I knew you'd understand. Now, the only thing I need to know – the only subject, I should say, on which I'd like some kind of assurance – is this. How closely can you tell the date of conception?'

Whatever you do, show nothing. Miranda said, 'Well, they must've given you an expected date of delivery. You can just work backwards from that, then add anything up to an extra week. For a first child.'

'For a first child, you say? So does that mean they could be guessing?' He was willing her to agree. Did he know anything about Julie's spare-time activities? Or was this just jealous insecurity?

The thought made her unwary, at least for as long as it took to say, 'Dad, if there's something you can't tell me—'

'No. Did I say that? Did I say anything that might make you think that?'

The shutters were down. In an instant she'd been reduced to an insolent stranger.

'I'm sorry; I should have been more indirect.'

'No,' he said. 'That's not good enough. You can't just say things like that and walk away.'

Was he actually about to stop her leaving the room? She slipped past him into the hall, hoping for a witness – anyone – to inhibit him.

'I didn't mean to offend you. Maybe I'd better go to bed.'

You Said She's Where?

How could she have humiliated him so carelessly? He shouted after her, 'But maybe not in my house.'

He might have meant it, if only to throw her out for that night. But at that moment Etta appeared. A questioning look all over her.

Evidently she didn't know that Miranda had moved in that week. 'Oh, are you staying? Of course if you've brought your own sheets, then there should easily be enough to go round.' To Adam she said, 'I suppose she'll have to go in the nursery, on the sofa bed.'

This too shook his pride. 'Miranda already sleeps there. It's to be her room for as long as she needs it.'

Was this really home once more? Not for the first time she found herself thinking, have I been got back here as some kind of spy? Watching Julie? Oh God, must I? Only later, in the moments before sleep when nonsense words form in one's head, would something said by Julie on the phone snag her memory. But that too was gibberish, without a context. Meanwhile she went upstairs to pass the night wrapped in sheets and blankets on a sofa bed she couldn't face unfolding, in a place made unrecognizable by wallpaper printed with fairies and toadstools and now in transit between an unborn child and a lost boy.

Thirty-seven

He could have been standing out there for half an hour. Watching her from two yards away. A ghost almost; a motionless holograph.

She had maybe heard a noise. Something ordinary, like a cat, maybe a squirrel. Even a fox, out to scavenge from the dustbins.

Her heart spasmed in pity at the sight of him.

'Joshie!' Miranda wrenched open the back door and ran to embrace him. However grown-up he sometimes pretended to be, she knew it was what Laura would have done.

He was unresisting and close to tears.

'Mandy. What shall I do?'

He spoke so low, she wasn't sure she heard him right. 'What? Joshie, what?'

'What shall I do, Mandy? Please help me.'

'Come inside,' she insisted, trying to guide him. As though he were a frail old man or a little boy.

'I'm not going in if any of them are there.' He put a dull, dogged emphasis on 'them'.

'No one's in except me.' It was Saturday and the house

was empty. 'Dad's off jogging, and Julie's out too; I don't know where.'

'She's with me.' He spoke as if scared to hear his own words.

'What?' she said, stupidly.

'At my place – she's in the squat.'

If Miranda hadn't followed him the other day she wouldn't have had a clue where he was talking about. She said, 'Over there – in, um, Boscastle House? Is that where you mean?'

He showed no surprise that she knew. 'Mandy, please help me. It only started happening just after she'd had a scrap with Dad. Otherwise she wouldn't even have made a pass at me.'

This time, at least, she had the sense not to say anything as idiotic as 'what?' She even managed not to sigh out loud. Bedding his stepmother. Well done, Josh. Another box ticked in the pursuit of trouble.

'I just couldn't see any reason to say no. After we ran into each other in the street. You know how that's like.' He was crying now, shaking with unashamed sobs. His nose ran.

'Sort of. Have this.' She reached to take the kitchen paper off its roller. Waited for whatever else he had to confess. She didn't dare probe or hurry him; nothing like being full of undefined dread to make you ask the wrong questions.

'Nothing would have gone wrong if I'd been there.'

'What? What's happened?' She could almost have wept too, out of sympathy with his hopeless state. And she wanted to hit him, from exasperation at not knowing what he meant.

'I think I know what happened. I just don't understand how.' He turned his face towards her in appeal, though in his overwrought state he might as well have been sightless. 'Mandy, it wasn't me!'

*

At least she was alive.

Once Josh had told her everything he could, Miranda knew what she wanted: to go and hide in the lavatory and lean her face against the cool tiled wall and shut her eyes until it had all gone away. Including him.

He'd found Julie in the squat, as their usual rendezvous. 'She liked to do it standing in the window, looking down at this place.'

She'd been conscious but someone had tied her up and gagged her.

'Someone?'

'Him. Whoever. She won't say.'

Miranda was on her feet, casting about for her bag and the keys to the household's runabout. 'Was she bleeding?'

'I don't think so. She just said she wanted to come back here and make some calls. Only, when I left to get you she was being sick.'

Miranda went and squatted down beside the chair where he sat. 'Joshie – look – I'll come with you; don't worry. But shouldn't we phone for help right away?'

'She said no. I said aren't you frightened and she just

said, no police. She probably thinks she might get done for possession.'

'At least you came to me.' For what that might be worth.

Thirty-eight

The lift was broken, which was a relief. It felt safer using the stairs. Safe from what, she didn't stop to think. Most flats seemed empty; certainly they were boarded up. Every so often you did hear voices, normal-sounding but sparse. One flat even had clean net curtains looped across its internal windows. Squatters came all sorts, Laura had once said, describing this very block. Some desecrate a place, others try to do it up a bit. Just as having them light a fire could either mean keeping out the damp or burning the place down.

Four floors up they came to where Josh had been living. He couldn't have thought he'd be staying long. The front door had two locks including a mortise, but he evidently found it quicker just to jemmy the top one open with an old credit card, then give the door a sharp nudge with his shoulder. The flat was furnished with little more than a mattress and a rubbish-tip sofa; it was hard to tell if the place was normally untidy or had recently been violently taken apart.

'She's in the bathroom.'

Miranda turned to run in there, but he stopped her. 'Mandy …'

'What? – Joshie – what, for God's sake?'

'Before you go in … Someone had gagged her, with her tights. And I took the handle of a sink plunger thing out of her. I know I shouldn't—'

'Out of her?' She wanted to shut a mental door on the possibilities.

He stood well back while Miranda went into the bathroom. Julie was curled up on the dusty lino floor, looking at the skirting board with the blank expression of waiting for something they knew would never happen; Josh had said she might have been well blasted beforehand. There was a bruise coming at the corner of her mouth. But to a quick glance, apart from a runny nose and the smell of puke there was no sign that anything dire had been done to her.

'Julie…'

She turned her head to look at Miranda. If she hadn't still been doped, she would surely have started to weep. An injured cat in her position would have let out a piteous miaow. As it was, she seemed to have no idea of herself as a wounded creature.

'I want to go home.'

'We've got the car. You can go straight to St Edmund's—'

'Nooo!' She pulled herself into a sitting position, twisting like a thing ensnared.

'At least let me call the police.'

'No, please!'

Miranda felt the same collision of anger and sympathy she'd suffered towards Josh. Pity made her want to dissolve down to the soles of her feet; and rage had her half choked that that these two morons had got her into this. Whatever it was.

She wanted out of here fast. Was this attack really a coincidence? Unconnected with Frances?

Or herself?

If it turned out that Julie needed hospitalization, she was going to call the emergency services and the hell with it. Miranda got Josh to pick his stepmother up in his arms while she took Julie's bag and shut the front door behind them. He looked self-conscious at having to do something so intimate as carrying Julie downstairs; it was hard to imagine that only recently they'd been going at it like weasels on speed. This particular reality had left them not fancying each other one bit.

Thank God there'd still be no one at the house. All the way home, driving white-knuckled over speed humps at twenty miles an hour, Miranda pictured Adam's fierce concern. His insistent questioning. After they'd got Julie upstairs and into bed, still fully clothed except for her shoes, she told Josh he'd better disappear. To keep in touch he'd call her at half-hour intervals until there was definite news of Julie's condition.

As the big front door shut behind him, she ran back upstairs. On the bed Julie was lying just as Miranda had found her in the squat: curled tight on her side and staring at nothing. She'd developed a frown of concentration, and Miranda wondered if coming down was bringing a paranoid spell.

She said Julie's name, as kindly as she could, though she was so angry-scared for both of them that no way could she have impersonated her ideal reassuring self. Julie didn't look up, but made a little mewing noise of acknowledgement.

'Did you know them – him – whoever it was?'

Like a child who can only understand one idea at a time, Julie said, 'My tummy hurts.'

She could have been describing one of several conditions. Miranda said, 'Does the pain come and go?'

Julie opened her mouth as if to answer. When not a word came out, Miranda realized she'd been struck dumb. People don't always respond to pain by crying out. Sometimes it leaves them too used up to make a sound.

Two minutes passed before Julie stopped looking wild-eyed. 'It's gone away.' She sounded surprised, as if the pain was something she'd expected to last forever.

'Julie – when's your expected date of delivery?'

'I'm four and a half months.' Her voice was faint and resigned.

After Miranda had phoned for an ambulance, she called Adam. She pictured him taking the call in his running things, standing half bent over among all the other joggers in Victoria Park. At first he just sounded breathless. As he recovered, anxiety made him adopt his workplace voice and rap out demands for an instant full debrief. By the time she'd told him everything she could, he'd reached his car and was on the way home.

Calling Etta felt worse – partly because it was bewildering. Knowing how far imagination can run ahead of the facts, Miranda started out with reassurances. But at the mention of hospitalization Julie's mother had breathed, '*What?*' – and then rung off without waiting for an answer.

Even with time sidling like a glacier it was a shock to see Etta arrive so soon. Hurrying in, she looked around the hallway as if the walls and ceiling could tell her more. Miranda almost felt she'd brought on the crisis herself.

Had she misjudged the woman? Etta really did look as if she felt for her daughter as much as for any other child of her own.

Adam arrived right behind, double-parking in his haste and leaving his lights blinking. He ran after Etta just in time to stop her closing the front door ahead of him.

'If you'll both forgive me …' he said. And ran ahead of them, taking the stairs two at a time.

Left waiting, Etta seemed not to notice how often she looked at her watch.

'The ambulance is bound to be here in the next twenty minutes.' Miranda had to say something reassuring.

Etta swivelled. She looked surprised, but also dismayed. 'You mean there's one coming now? Are you sure?'

'I'm sorry?'

'You haven't sent for one yet, have you?'

'Well, yes. At this stage of pregnancy it's an offence in law to leave someone without proper help if they're miscarrying. It's not just like an extra heavy menstruation.'

'But she is only going into hospital to be put under observation?' It sounded like a command rather than a question.

'Perhaps. Look, I really am sorry—'

'So there's no question of any operation? Or an investigation – the kind that would need a general anaesthetic?'

'She might need a D and C – a scrape – to make sure of a straightforward recovery. I do understand how—'

'But that might not be necessary? She could choose? Maybe if she went to the right hospital?'

'There is no right hospital,' Miranda said angrily. 'The treatment is the same everywhere, depending on what's needed.'

'But if it were needed – could she not have a local anaesthetic?'

'If you're worried about the risks of a general one, they really do amount to nothing. Specially when compared to avoiding treatment altogether. I'm sure the people doing it would want to reassure you themselves—'

'I'm not concerned on my own account.' She made such an idea sound idiotic. 'But I know my daughter would be mortified by the thought of any indignity.'

'They do try and make the patient's identity as invisible they can.' Miranda started to explain the details, but Etta cut her short again.

'My daughter has every right to be self-conscious about saying meaningless things. In the hearing of strangers.'

'But – no – people are so used to it – she really...' For God's sake shut up, Miranda told herself as her imagination thronged with dire possibilities.

Adam hurried in. The sight of him. Anyone's heart would have contracted in sympathy.

Miranda went up to him. You wouldn't want to raise

your voice all the way across the room – not at someone looking like that. 'Dad? Do you want me to call the police?'

He looked panicked, more than grieved. 'That won't be necessary.'

It was no time to hassle anyone in his state of mind. But she couldn't help asking, 'Are you sure?'

'We can think about that later.'

'Quite,' Etta said with emphasis. She threw a tentative look at Adam, as though assessing him.

The doorbell sounded. Both of them started, as if it was the last thing they'd expected. But now that the ambulance crew was here, at least it seemed that for whatever reason Etta dared not say another word.

Thirty-nine

In the canteen at St Ted's Miranda was trying to eat a buttered roll and some minestrone. But her mouth felt as dry as if she'd died and turned to dust. Now that Julia's pregnancy was lost, followed in surgery by a D and C, she was waiting to know if after Etta and Adam she too could go in and visit.

For weeks – months, now – a life of normality had been a vanishing memory, back in its lost land of Before. So what that no crisis or calamity had been her fault? Any more than if a piece of aircraft wreckage had fallen on her from six miles up while she was at home watching the telly.

Fat lot of comfort that was. What if the police did get involved? Even if she could guess what questions they'd ask, who knew what Julie might say, true or false? With distress leaving her mind at its weakest? Or fear making her ruthless in whatever story she was led to tell?

Right now Etta was with her; and who knew what was being said between mother and daughter? Only last week, in a potential stinker of a scene, Etta had tried to accuse Josh of theft after Julie, brain-fogged as hell, had sought in vain throughout the house for one of her handbags – a dainty piece of work, French-blue patent leather lined with biscuit-coloured suede. Etta's response was immediate: 'Some people,' she told Miranda, 'should realise that they can't just go and give anyone access to the family home.'

She meant of course the copied key Miranda had given her brother – more as a gesture of support than handing over anything he'd want to use.

Etta had trembled with dour excitement as she added, 'Because other people might be led to think it looks like the act of an accomplice.'

White-faced with astonishment, Miranda had had no chance to point out that she knew where the damned handbag was, having just agreed to take it for mending. It had been at this moment that Adam had come in through the front door and passed upstairs. He'd murmured a greeting at Miranda but made no acknowledgement of Etta – who'd responded to his presence nonetheless by bolting out of sight. Eyes lowered, as she'd morphed on the spot into the essence of female submission.

What the hell? Something to do with the marriage? God alone knew. But recently there'd been another first. Richard had stayed overnight a couple of times at a more-or-less invitation from her father. Adam had even made a show of inviting him to share his own master-bathroom, careless of whether or not he'd take a professional snoop at the medicine cabinet and its tale of newly faltering middle age. Etta might once have been righteous at Richard's expense, as if denouncing a housemaid's followers. Now it seemed she dare not.

In the hospital cafeteria a glass wall separated

Miranda's table from the ground floor's main corridor. It was obvious, now she saw Thomas in the distance, that he must have been Julie's first visitor. Coming closer, hunched and striding, he seemed to sense nothing of his surroundings. He passed within a yard of Miranda as though she, like all the hurrying people around him, was a ghost.

Seeing him, she would have tried to be invisible anyway. His handsome face was disfigured by weeping, but that was the least of it. Though any heart would've clenched in pity, there was a look about him that could have made strong men fear to meet his eye.

What in God's name might have happened, up in surgery? When, moments later, Etta came in and bustled up to her, Miranda was apprehensive enough to get to her feet. She braced herself to say something without the least idea what was needed: hope, reassurance, even shock and condolence?

'Please don't get up. Things are concerning enough for you as it is. And it's so kind of you to wait around to see my daughter.'

Who was this total stranger?

'…I just wanted to reassure you that everything will work out for her. Physically, that is.'

Miranda found her voice. Stopped staring, even.

'That's really good to hear. So—?'

'But I simply dread the effect of this for my son. I'm sure even his friends here would be surprised at him – however well he conceals it. All his life he's been such a sensitive boy. People just won't understand what a burden it is to feel everything as strongly as he does… I'm worried for that girl too. Perhaps you'll understand – you especially, no doubt – when I say his sister wants only to forget – to put everything behind her. I know how disappointed you'll be; but today she's really not equal to seeing any more visitors. "Mum," she said to me just now, "all I want is for everyone to be discreet."'

Soon after, having delivered her masterclass in emollience, she left. So earnest was her parting look of sincerity that for one queasy moment Miranda thought they were supposed to air-kiss.

But as she got up to go home one thing said by Etta now stood forth as huge and welcoming as a Statue of Liberty.

'Of course, like Thomas and me, my daughter is adamant that no charges are brought.'

Never mind whether in some alternative universe there was such a counterfactual creature as Adamant Julie. For Miranda, just hearing the words almost transfigured the luckless girl's mother into an angel of deliverance. Reasonably or not, it cast all sorts of things in a hopeful light. If she herself was suddenly Goody Two-Shoes, could this mean Josh too was clear of trouble? Safely unsuspected all along of his dumb adventure with Julie? And back in the Square with its recent associations, dismal or fraught, she was stopping just long enough to collect the last of her stuff for the trip to America. Then off to supper with Richard before they each made their booking. It'll only be a holiday, she told herself…

Jostled by ordinary troubles – money, family – had she

let herself imagine demonic malice where there was none? Maybe the severed hand and the text message received in mid-air were just a sick practical joke. From someone ordinary like the two boys at Josh's school who'd grabbed a classmate's visiting girlfriend and pushed her into an ornamental pond for a joke, then jumped in themselves and pushed her under several times. It was Founder's Day, and the national dailies took it up in a big way, as if only nice people got admitted to posh schools. Why did you do it? they were asked afterwards. Scared as hell at finding themselves in serious trouble they'd muttered, 'Because we liked her.'

Could that be what she was up against? Someone too stupid even to know if they meant harm? The thought was liberating – as far as it went. The girl who got ducked had nearly died. In front of a crowd of pupils and visiting parents it had taken two ashen-faced staff members a serious effort to revive her.

But in vain she told herself not to cheer up. Besides, there was another thing Etta had just said, whose significance was now brightening and expanding like a summer sunrise.

'My daughter is resolved to have a change of scene.'

'Oh?' Resolute Julie just sounded like another mythical beast. But—

'I'm taking her away for a while. Back to her home environment.'

'Home?' Where, for God's sake? Surely for Etta's offspring childhood had been defined by serial displacement, not homecomings.

Somewhere in America, it seemed. 'There she can get back to being herself. After this ghastly recent outcome.'

*

Being driven back to the Maida Vale apartment Etta was preoccupied to the point that the world outside the taxi's windows seemed as irrelevant as a wraparound film screen. Throughout that day one harrying thought had cast a shadow over everything.

How could that girl have been so stupid?

Another anonymous offering from her in-box. A piece of film like the others. Almost.

So far nothing had threatened Etta herself. She'd always known that; and counted on it.

But for God's sake. In the marital bed!

This mating had been different in more than one way. Any stranger might have found it touching; intimate for one thing, unlike any of the other encounters filmed so far. It bore a sense of two halves made whole by a comradeship fit to last a married couple forever. Into a distant old age sweetened by laughing at their surviving togetherness like a pair of successful conspirators.

Seeing this, Etta felt neither compassion nor moral dishevelment. Her mind was focused on practicalities, alert as a rat sniffing the inside of an unsuspected trap. As before, both naked bodies were on show. The curtain might nonetheless have hidden their identities from most onlookers; not from her. She'd always had suspicions – but now, even without the soundtrack, murmurous and down-to-earth, she'd have known them both. She, of all people.

*

Miranda made her way back to Albany Square feeling like the lead actor in an upbeat movie of her own life. Even the empty house felt like a character in its own right: the dependable best friend perhaps, in a romcom. 'Idiot,' she said, running upstairs to her room. Aloud, chiding herself at her own good humour. But still smiling as she spoke.

But then she paused, for a moment almost forgetting why she was there. What caught her imagination was the silence in the house, bringing to mind how it usually sounded. A background of electronic noise: radio, vacuuming, work in the garden. Adam taking a shower; Julie on the phone.

Last week, when her father had asked her if she'd move in. Julie, half out of earshot, murmuring into the phone with bred-in-the-bone familiarity. Her voice had had none of its usual social trill; she'd been down to earth, serious. No wonder her altered tone had snagged Miranda's attention in another room.

It wasn't just that. There was the name she'd used.

'Only you, Mr Glad Pig.'

For God's sake! The videos. In Miranda's mind any question about identity had been getting dulled and meaningless through sheer repetition.

Not anymore.

Often the likeliest answer isn't found by thrashing

about in search of it. Instead it seeks you out, unbidden. For no reason she could see, one figure strode to mind. Ravaged by God knew what dismay, At the hospital.

Thomas St Clair. She would have exclaimed out loud.

Except—

That was when they let themselves in.

Well, why not here?

Forty

Kitty

Each of us secretly knew how we most feared to die. Anyone who's said otherwise is lying.

But here? In this dignified provincial old mansion, with its well-ordered household?

I didn't have to be here. But some of the others had insisted: 'Trust us.' And you had to trust people. That's why we'd agreed to meet in this way: someone we'd trusted had started betraying people. Then I'd been contacted by that extraordinary woman who'd managed all too briefly to place herself in the local department of depositions.

When she'd passed on to me the name used by the informer, I'd wept with relief.

As I was let into the house, then into the study, at first all I saw was that only three of them were there.

'What's happened?' I looked stupidly around the room. 'What's gone wrong?'

Where was the man we'd planned to decoy to this place?

They stood facing me. Yves, sick with revulsion and

suspense; Leclair willing himself to give me a hard look; Arnault glancing at me, implacable. Maybe I willed myself for a moment not to see the gun, trained by Arnault onto its target.

The traitor was here, sitting in the big chair with its back to the door. He made himself look up at me. Hopelessly, as if from the bottom of his own grave.

And yes. It was Lucien.

It was obvious now: he himself must already have been betrayed. He'd been bound to turn informer if, say, the authorities had threatened his mother and his sister.

We all knew why we were here. And that somehow the deed must be done quietly. Arnault and Leclair resumed whispering between themselves in a rage of urgency.

The knock on the door produced a silence as sudden and loud as lifting the needle from a gramophone.

Lucien's mother looked into the room. I swear she saw nothing. All along she can't have known a thing. Lucien would have made sure of that, for her sake.

'Bonjour, messieurs. Bonjour, Catherine.'

'Bonjour, madame.'

Seeing that she'd interrupted something, she made her excuses to Lucien. '… Later, then?'

'Yes. Thank you, maman.'

Elsewhere Lucien's sister, fifteen, carefully reared, was doing her piano practice. She was mastering an old Christmas carol: 'Il est né, le divin enfant…' You couldn't help noticing how well she played. Ever since, that tune has been the most terrible sound I can think of.

You Said She's Where?

*

Well, why not here? Why not in the place Miranda had once seen as ultimate safety? From the start they would've had access.

And now. Prone, passive, knowing that soon rather than late they'd come back in and watch her piss herself from dread. And outside, through all of it, the rapture of the blackbird's song.

The moment when she saw the hypodermic. If only she hadn't been told what was in it.

If only she hadn't lost hope – if they'd cared whether she recognized them. But now all she wanted was to reach the end.

She knew Thomas St Clair now for what he was in every way. Not just the demented stalker who'd threatened her without reason but someone wanting to savour his own deeds to the limit. Where the other man – boy rather – lingered in the background like a common gawper at a public execution, St Clair shimmered with wounded righteousness. She – or someone close to her – was supposed to have done him wrong? Was that why he'd wanted to draw out the experience?

Either way she had to be punished.

He did what he'd come to do, with a show of deftness and a tight look of containment meant to shame her into feeling vulgar and out of control.

Afterwards, putting the syringe away, he went on looking her in the eye. And something happened that astonished her.

She stared back. Now that they'd done what they

threatened, she was suddenly free not to fear them. She knew the worst, right down to every symptom.

But then he reached out and seized her by the jaw. His grasp barely trembled as he turned her face towards him; but she knew he couldn't go on much longer looking perfectly deliberate. At the moment of physical contact with him, her own blissed-out rage was gone. All too well she pictured how she'd soon be, whether or not he planned some extra harm.

A sudden noise made her lurch in the chair as if electrocuted. Several milliseconds passed before she realized it was only the phone. After four rings Julie's recorded tones fluted through the empty room next door: '…but…dum-de-dum…we're really not here right now – honestly…'

St Clair stood and looked away at the sound of his sister's voice. Abstracted, like someone waiting for the national anthem to finish.

Then, from the ansaphone, a response in real time. 'Mandy …' Richard, sounding happy; you could hear his unconscious smile. 'Nothing to worry about. But since you don't seem to be there I'll call later…'

After his voice was gone she wept: noisy, fat, blubbering, snot-provoking tears that left her caring for nothing but what caused them. She was two people: the calm observer of her own grief, and the helpless creature lost to everything but the sorrow of what must be about to happen.

From somewhere behind her she heard their muttered conference.

'Fuck it.' The other man, the apparent sidekick. Rattled

by the phone's intrusion. 'I mean, see the state of that?' meaning her. 'We're done here, aren't we?'

'Just a few minutes… look, trust me. This is what we agreed, okay?'

'If you reckon. But it won't look too good, like all trussed up. Better untie it before we go.'

'No problem. This one here knows what symptoms to expect.' Then louder, in her ear, 'Isn't that right, Miranda?' Her name spoken as if she'd no claim to be called anything. His desperate face, almost out of sight, straining with the righteous rage that had somehow brought him to this.

Almost out of sight, but now slowly revolving past her, over and over.

'Dizziness, yes. Right on time.' A hand that knew its business, taking her pulse. 'And this is responding how it should…'

After she'd been untied, he squatted in front of her. She kept her eyes shut, wanting in vain to be sick again.

'Now, you know the reaction time. Don't you?' When she said nothing, he leaned closer. '*Don't you?*'

She grunted, breathing hard. The thought occurred to her: all these symptoms coincide with those of terror. How stupid, if she'd been injected with nothing more than distilled water or some harmless behaviour-adjusting drug and just died of fright.

'So,' he insisted, 'does this mean you could still have had a chance? Given time.'

She tried shaking her head, to show she couldn't easily say anything. It made the repeated sliding movement of the room a lot worse.

'You don't have to speak; that's not what I mean – Yeah, right away—' to the other man, who'd said something from halfway down the stairs. 'But hey, where's your sense of humour, Miranda? You can still kid yourself this is just a joke. Say, an excess of something personality-enhancing? Harmless enough, if a bit of a sod in the mean time. Die hoping, like a loser; why don't you?

'Not a joke with Frances. When you killed her.' Her tongue felt and sounded like a gag.

'I'll be the judge of that.'

She tried in vain to say something else. The only sound she could manage seemed detached from her; the noise of some nearby beast. The roaring of blood in her head threatened to wipe out any other sensation, together with the certainty that at any moment she'd faint. If only the last experience in her life didn't have to be the sound of Thomas St Clair's voice.

He stood up to go. As he did so she found that despair still fought with something else – something unreasoning – to overmaster her. Alone at last, crawling, eyes shut against nausea, she fought to grasp a pencil and write on the wall. A single diagnostic word. Collapsing onto her elbows, then bumping her head against the skirting board; she couldn't afford to wait until they were quite gone. The heavy front door did close. But only after St Clair's parting words, shouted from downstairs but heard incoherently, as if originating in her own skull.

'Goodbye Miranda. Have a nice death.'

Forty-one

Kitty

His mother left us, satisfied that all was well. Lucien turned his face towards me. Seeing me, he'd registered a moment of horror. But now, taking my hand, he looked up at me.

'I know you acted in ignorance.' Lacking privacy, he spoke in English: something he'd never done before. I tried to avoid his eyes, but he only pulled me closer. 'You must believe what I tell you when I say you acted for the best.'

It could have been anyone's – that damned alias I'd passed on.

I couldn't speak. I'd always feared for him so much.

'In God's name,' he said to the others, 'let her go outside.'

*

The Range Rover with the tinted windows sidled out of the Square. Its windscreen cast back a reflection of Richard's car as he drove past.

He was early after all and supposed he'd have to wait before Miranda got back. What he ought to do was go downstairs and start making notes from the new term's recommended reading. Several things put him off making the effort. The evening was warm and luminous, the city itself just made for cruising along in his father's borrowed Saab, past all the people sitting outside cafés or spilling from crowded pubs.

He'd noticed the Range Rover right away, even though the Square wasn't short on that semi-armoured kind of family motor, heavy as Roman chariots. As it passed him a window was sliding up, with the driver briefly visible: young and incongruously scruffy. Mere curiosity made Richard glance at him. If the windows had been transparent he wouldn't have bothered. The man didn't return his look but stared straight ahead. Almost, at such close range, like someone who meant to be invisible.

Except …

At the last moment, about to leave the Square, the driver involuntarily cast a look upwards and back, towards the house he must have just left. His passenger was a vague shape: someone looking for his seat belt. There was nothing special for the driver to see; that was what seized Richard's attention. Without stopping to reason it out, he tried to intuit why the man had thrown that wary glance at Miranda's home. It astonished him that people did such things, giving themselves away with a gesture as fleeting as the click of a camera. Whoever the man was, the one thought provoked by him had been …?

*

You Said She's Where?

Kitty

They were panicked, Arnault and Leclair. 'You said we needed to be quick. How the hell are we supposed to get clear in time?'

'Who do you think will interrupt us now? No one else is coming in here.'

Lucien cut across their hissing noises of desperation. 'In the name of God,' he said again, 'whatever you do, let Catherine go now!'

'She stays,' Arnault said. 'Or if you prefer, we can get your mother and your sister in here as well.'

In his way he too had once loved Lucien. Only, jealously.

He passed the gun to one of the others and took from his pocket a length of cord. He still couldn't meet Lucien's eye as he went to stand behind him.

Lucien's last words. An order, if you like, calmly given. Holding me in his eyes.

'Catherine, don't look.'

So I turned my face away, and made it a point of honour not to flinch nor weep aloud. But they couldn't have made me let go of his hand. I held it even more tightly when, after a while, he shat himself. It must have been a long time before there was no further sign of life. But I'd clung on even when I'd thought his grasp would break my bones.

*

The senses don't all have to go at once: often they close down one by one. Soon she could no longer see colours, nor movement nor shapes, but only darkness and light; then these too faded fast, to where there was only hearing, faint and incoherent.

Richard could never afterwards bring himself to describe in detail the full horror of her final moments of consciousness and beyond. The uncertainty of whether her last gasped-out mutterings completed the word she'd wanted to scrawl. The no-other-hope gamble of thrusting through the contents of Adam's bathroom cabinet amid the sound of breaking glass to find the sympathomimetic drug he'd seen there before. The violence with which he'd wrestled her into choking down a massive dosage; one that might still be in time to save her or, if his guessed-at diagnosis was wrong, would kill her outright.

No one was ever to hear just what passed through his mind during those minutes of frenzy and shouting aloud at no one. Most certain of all was that she never would.

Forty-two

Kitty

The snowfields were full of strange sounds. A crowd in a sports arena, whose noise swelled and faded like the breath of one creature. At the highest pass, a full peal of church bells. After that, faint at first, there grew the sense of someone unseen, walking beside me.

On one snowy traverse, streaked with trails of fallen boulders, Lucien was waiting. He was dressed for summer, in corduroy trousers and a short-sleeved shirt. Without speaking he turned and led the way. The dun-coloured air bristled with flurries of fine snow.

Sometimes after that I seemed to be alone; at others the rest of our group of refugees were there. The only constant was Lucien, walking ahead. After a while I began to hear his voice in my head, patiently commanding me to keep walking. Once, lagging behind, I found myself on the ground, with snow clogging my mouth and freezing on my eyebrows: I'd slipped and winded myself.

Lucien was hunkered down and waiting, just beyond the people standing round me till I got my breath back.

Even while feeling as if all my internal organs had come loose, I knew why he looked the way he did. This was a flashback.

Last summer we'd been walking through the local Forêt de Domaine. The pathway back had been steep and muddy, fording boulder-strewn rivulets. At one place I'd slipped and my feet shot from under me. Lucien had called out, quick but unfussed, 'Catherine, don't move,' before turning back to join me.

So that's how the next few minutes had passed. He, squatting beside me where I'd fallen; I, supported on one elbow and trying to breathe easily. Above us, specks of light shifting in the forest canopy. If I could bear it I suppose that's how I'd always want to think of us, together in our bubble of solitude, each thinking our own thoughts ...

I shouldn't even be writing this. But after what I did, at least no one will ever hear me speak of him. For the rest of my life.

One other thing I got wrong. Just before he died. I never told him I might be pregnant.

Forty-three

She dreamed she was coming back into the world. In reality wasn't she leaving it? How could any return to life be so vague and repetitive?

The after-effects of dichlorophene can do that when combining with its own antidotes; so Miranda read later. At first every part of her was too heavy to move, like she was a giant fallen to earth. Yet she was floating too: a benign, carefree sensation, which was why she'd wondered if she was dying after all. The light was confusing, which would have bothered her if anything could. It seemed to have no source, yet come from everywhere.

After a while, people, all of whom she knew, began fading in and out of sight. She couldn't believe how many hospital staff seemed to be there at one time or another. At first she couldn't tell which encounters were genuine. Julie's haggard presence was surely an illusion; later though, someone else confirmed the reality of at least one ghostlike visitation. Presumably including the look of sincerity, breathy and wide-eyed, in which she seemed to speak of 'you know, like putting all this behind me'.

DC Rosa Hill, coming and going, eventually resolved

into such a frequent presence that she had to be real. One morning when the sunlight spilling in made every outline blurry she sat by the bed and told Miranda something about St Clair and his co-villain. Later, falling asleep in mid-morning, Miranda dreamed a dream in which the two of them transformed from fiery wicker men into harmless human-shaped haycocks.

Later, fast recovering, she had a visitor whom she was shocked not to have recognized at first. He was wearing a hospital-issue dressing gown and hadn't combed his hair or shaved. It was a terrible thing, to mistake her own father for some cleaned up street drunk who'd blundered into her room by accident. Her first response had been to reach for the panic button, on its long flex by the bed like a outsize computer mouse. Then she remembered that the police guard on her room had been proved superfluous, long before she'd known they'd been there.

By now she was able to sit up. She still felt dreamily passive, but also like some wondrous marionette too fragile to be used without breakage. A sense of illusion – a glamour spell – still came off everything: the plastic bedside beaker, even the glass jars and other improvised containers holding flowers from the stall outside the hospital's main gate. The feeling was heightened by seeing Adam, in this public place, dressed in a tatty robe as for Sunday breakfast back in the Square.

There'd been another reason why Adam looked like a chronic drinker. He'd turned an unfamiliar shade of red, one you wouldn't have got from the most over-ambitious game of squash.

'Dad?'

'How are you, lovey?' He sat down slowly, as if the bedside chair might bruise him.

'Dad? ... Are you here as one of Mr Urquhart's patients?'

He gave a dismissive gesture. 'The man's imagining things.'

'Probably not. He's well rated.'

'That's as may be.' He'd evidently forgotten that he'd just asked after her. Not because he didn't care, but because his own woes bore down on him. He paused, like someone briefly aware that they've had one too many.

Then he launched forth. 'The fact is, hearts don't break literally. Not that mine is fractured in any sense.' He was trying to speak in a measured way; but his hands shook. 'The woman doesn't exist who could do that to me. Thinks I haven't yet struck her out of my will? Does she, by God!' Anger was stalking him, prodding him this way and that like a cat with a captured vole.

'I'm sorry if you're not happy.'

It was a cue – a query – that he couldn't ignore. That much was clear from the denunciations that now spurted from him. Some of his language was traditional enough to be quaint; the rest was just the foul banalities you'd get in any A & E unit on a busy Saturday night.

'Strumpet. Harlot. Drab. Jade. Mopsy... Rutting cunt. Cunt...' Tears stood in his eyes.

Though pity and revulsion elbowed each other, she didn't feel strong enough. Not for an incontinent unburdening like this: from the first fleeting instant when Julie had been inattentive to his lovemaking, through to some half-audible phone conversations, in a voice he'd thought she only used with himself. All the way up to when, eavesdropping, he heard, 'Oh, it's him. I've got to go.'

He leaned forward. 'But Mandy, *you* must have known how it was for me. You were the only person there who understood. I could hardly wait for you to move back home.' He paused, then said, 'You know I've restored your allowances to you both, don't you?'

'No?' Miranda looked back at him; for a moment, struck dumb. Josh too? His dumb adventure with Julie unsuspected?

'Aren't you pleased?'

'Of course I am. It's just rather a shock.' Surprise apart, the relief was too great to be sensed all at once. Later, perhaps, his news would feel as good as it deserved. Like sliding into a warm bath after months of sleeping rough.

One question that couldn't be left out. 'But Dad – you're planning to separate?'

He was about to say something when one of the nurses came in then hesitated, seeing a visitor.

'It's okay, thanks, Kelly.'

The nurse went ahead with checking blood pressure and pulse rate, while Miranda and her father froze in mid-exchange.

When she'd left, Adam turned and hissed, 'Well, what do you think we're doing?' In a low voice as if in danger of being overheard, he vented another toxic surge of expletives.

'…Lecherous, treacherous, incestuous… *bint*…

Insolent bint. Didn't have the common decency to deny a damn thing. After that all I need do was follow her. She thought I was that other cunt, coming in… What? What?… You think I give a flying fuck who the cunt was?'

Miranda struggled not to look wary. 'If you mean what I think, the man's not at large any more…'

Then another, hideous thought assailed her.

It was you! You did that to her. The words stood forth, unutterable.

'Mandy…' He tried to lay a hand on her arm. 'I know you've always appreciated my point of view. You have understood me, haven't you?'

'All too well, now.'

There'd been times in the last few months when she'd fantasized about Adam turning to her for help or sympathy. Now all she felt was a weight of melancholy, making her judgment harsh and filling her eyes with tears of disillusionment.

'What do you want?'

'Look. We can help each other.' He glanced at the closed door.

She guessed right away what he meant.

'No, Dad, we can't.'

It wasn't hard to picture his state of mind as he'd followed Julie to the squat. Not knowing whether he wanted to plead or get revenge. On her or the unknown Other.

'You want me to say it can't have been you. That I was somewhere with you all the time.'

'Darling… Look, you know how these things can

sometimes turn out for the worst. Whatever the truth of the underlying facts.'

How like him to hear only what he wanted. Her head ached; it felt heavy, as if her brain had been replaced with a facsimile in wet cement.

'Look, if you're in any trouble, I'm sorry. But I'm not going to pervert the course of justice, if that's what it takes to cover for you.'

At that moment she'd never seen him so frightened; not even back at home when the ambulance came for Julie. In vain he tried merely to look heavy with anger. Nearly half a minute went by while neither spoke. Then, carefully, only of other things.

Forty-four

Over several careers Etta's massive powers of damage limitation had never been challenged as now. But true to a sense of her own latest identity, already she planned a self-reinvention to surpass them all: back in America with Julie as the media-useable child of her bosom. No way had she cause for either of them to linger. Here, overseas?

*

[Fade up studio applause]
[Imelda Zieff]: And now welcome back to the show for the second part of our unique interview with the amazing Etta St Clair, newly starring in The Etta St Clair Hour, 'the show that really does go all the way to the truth'. And here too with us this morning is her daughter Julie.

So, Etta, after the recent events in your life, how does it feel to be back in the good old US of A?

[E. St C.] It feels good. And you know why? Because for both me and my daughter, it's not just coming home to America: it's a return to American values. *[Applause]* Let's take what my daughter's just been through.

No one in our family believes in divorce. So when it was shown to us that her marriage to a glamorous Englishman was fated not to last, she knew at once where she had to be, to change her life back into something good. We all make mistakes, maybe even more when we find ourselves away from home, say in a foreign land like Europe. But afterwards my daughter and I knew, with total certainty, that the one place we wanted to be was America.

[Applause]

[**I. Z.**]: But what about your son? You must miss him so much.

[E. St C. pauses]

[**I. Z.**]: It's all right, Etta. Take your time. I can promise you that every person watching you here today is your friend.

[**E. St C.**]: Well, Imelda, I have to tell you this: the one thing that has helped me through my ordeal has been the love and support of my viewers. There are so many truly wonderful people out there who understand. They really do. They know that if the hand of fate has made you suffer, then one day your grief is bound to strengthen you.

[**I. Z.**]: That is so true! *[To audience]* Don't you agree?

[Loud applause]

And Etta, wouldn't you say too that this has deepened what you personally have to offer all your viewers. Hasn't it has helped you to face the troubles of many of your TV guests as profoundly as we all know you do?

[**E. St C.**]: Truly it has. And – I have to tell you this, since in so many ways sharing is what I feel I was born to do – let me just tell you all here today that what my family and I have been through was always bound to make us closer. Yes, even the doubts I had at the time about whether I'd really done my duty as a mother.

[**I. Z.**]: Such as …?

[**E. St C.**]: I know this sounds silly, but somehow it's the little things that come back to haunt your conscience. Like the time my daughter's birthday came round and to my horror I found there wasn't the right wrapping paper for her presents. Because, you see, the only giftwrap we had was Christmas paper – you know, with snowmen all over it. But to my relief, do you know, she was as good as gold about it.

[**I. Z.**]: And, Julie, when this happened, what did you say to your mother?

[**J. St C.**]: I said, 'That's all right, Mum.' *[Prolonged laughter and applause]*

[**I. Z.**]: So, Etta, I think we can say there was always a good chance that whatever the setbacks the years since then might hold for you both, in the end they could only bring you closer together.

[**E. St C.**]: That's right. Bad things do happen. But, you know, that's how we find the good in ourselves. That's how we learn to rise up, to what we know we deserve.

[**Z. Z.**]: And Julie: we all know that these have been specially difficult times for you. What do you feel about your recent experiences?

[**J. St C.**]: I agree with Mum. *[Laughter and applause]*....

*

I'm not blaming anyone of mine. Even now, here. What if things had been different when we were growing up? That's the thing most people say now. Bewilderment, they say, was the one thing she and I could count on sometimes. But that's how I could help her. To be everything to her, even when we were small.

Now we're more than ever a couple; no matter how far away she is, nor who she's with. If anyone thinks of the so-called marriage at all, she's the one they'll remember, with him merely in the background. And all because of me; because I chose it like that. To make the world see how much I'd do for us both.

I know what he did to her. At the hospital she told me

everything. She could still go public about him if I told her to. I would have made her, straight away, if I hadn't stopped to think.

Not that it didn't cost me, holding off for the sake of something better.

I still want him dead.

Though what would even be the point of that, if I couldn't do it with my own hands. Guns are no good; they're too impersonal. And it's not that he has to go slowly. I just want the intimacy of being up to my elbows in him.

Meanwhile it's better this way. Making him wonder: will he be safe?

Keeping control. That makes a difference, in a place like this.

And the main thing: making him see what a sideshow he was in her life. Now no one can say I haven't shown him.

Forty-five

Beyond the open window the trees above Upping Combe stood motionless as an Old Master, beneath a sky washed with early-autumnal blue. The country quiet magnified the racket of Josh's electric clippers where he was trimming the yew hedge down in the kitchen garden.

Before flying to visit Richard in the States, Miranda still had enough left of the summer vac to finish clearing out Kitty's things. The job she'd avoided till last was sorting an unappealing deposit of old paper. It lay in the bottom of a mahogany wardrobe that leaned away from the wall of Kitty's former bedroom as if frozen in motion. When Miranda was little she'd always been afraid to cross the sloping floor in front of it, in case it fell on top of her.

Starting in on a slurry of torn folders and loose yellowed pages, she found one pile of stuff that was scarcely dusty at all. Photo albums, all in good condition. Opening them at random she saw they included a record of the almost-present. More than one snapshot showed her in the shirt and jeans she wore today.

Her parents' family albums. She thought they'd been lost forever. Here was Adam, cheerfully looking as if flour-bombed and helping her and three-year-old Josh to make an apple crumble. Then Josh at about the same age, proudly wearing a newspaper hat fashioned for him by his father. And here was her brother, still little, and full of glee, sitting between their parents in the big bed with its view into a springtime garden. One photo was loose and fell out onto the floor. It was the sort of picture you find on most amateur rolls, the snap that nobody really meant to take. Usually it was an accidental shot of a skirting board or the photographer's knees. This one showed the dark blue and rose-coloured Afghan rug by her parents' bed, littered with clothes and shoes. Miranda put it back with the others, resolving to ask Kitty how she'd come by all these benign, heart-wringing souvenirs.

Most other stuff on the wardrobe floor looked as incoherent and pointless as you'd expect. There were electricity bills lying around loose, fifteen years out of date. Envelopes, now empty, posted to this address with the image of George VI on the stamp. A pack of Christmas cards, sent almost as long ago, exploded out of Miranda's grasp when the rubber band around them broke.

It was hard to figure at first if anything might be important. These ancient Christmas cards, say; one or two might well have been signed by someone famous. And buried under so much seeming rubbish was an old-fashioned leather briefcase, the kind that folds over itself to fasten. Mostly it held mementoes of Kitty's life around Miranda's own age: post-war correspondence from one or two publishers and from newspapers, some of them now extinct; news clippings in French; a torn brown envelope, unsealed, holding some negligently treated medals.

No way was Miranda prepared to make snap judgements about binning or keeping stuff like this. She pulled out another briefcase, shaped like a miniature Gladstone bag. Knowing Kitty's chaotic substitute for housekeeping, this was probably empty; wasted space in which some of these heaped-up documents could be taken away for storage.

In fact it was full, with just the one item: a box file closed with a spring. Inside the file everything was tidy, as if packed ready to lie there undisturbed for a lifetime. More carefully than before, Miranda turned its contents over, page by page.

Forged ration cards in French. One showed Kitty, easily recognizable from familiar studio photos of her as a teenager. It was strange to see her likeness above a fictitious name. Another had belonged to a man: young, with dark hair and a pale face. His name, even if it was his own, meant nothing to Miranda; neither here, nor on a Wanted poster, meticulously wrapped in cellophane, where his likeness, coarsened by cheap printing, accompanied a different ID.

Had Kitty come by these documents after the war? Or had she valued them so much that she'd taken the risk of carrying them back as a fugitive?

Beneath them, creases sharpened by having been undisturbed since the first half of last century, lay the answer to questions Miranda had never dreamed she should ask. Still staring at it, she got to her feet. Another, incredulous glance, and she was running, the fragile piece

You Said She's Where?

of paper fluttering in her hand as she scuttered down the twisting staircase and out into the sunlight.

Beside the raspberry canes at the far side of the garden, Josh saw her and turned off the hedge trimmer. As if nothing important was happening, she couldn't help noticing how neglected the garden had become; the air around him was full of motionless thistledown. Without saying anything she held out the paper.

Here, whoever else he'd been, was the real identity of the Frenchman with a reward on his head. His name, with Kitty's, was given on their child's adoption certificate. Two signatures belonged to Josh and Miranda's grandmother, Kitty's sister Margaret, and to Victor, their grandfather, as the new parents. The newborn infant was also named.

Baby Laura.

They'd always known their mother had been adopted. The date of birth was familiar, too.

Josh turned to look at her, likewise saying nothing.

*

Back in Kitty's old bedroom Miranda squatted on the floor and surveyed the muddle of remaining possessions. Two things – their mother's adoption certificate and the accidental-seeming photo that had fallen on the floor – now unexpectedly fused in her mind to form another question.

Or the beginnings of a question. Not yet knowing what she sought, Miranda excavated the most recent album from the pile where she'd stacked it, and took out the photo.

Two and a half minutes, she'd once read, was how long it took to notice everything in even the most cluttered movie shot. There wasn't nearly so much in this picture. She could possess its secret, if there was one, in seconds.

A lot was familiar. The clothes tossed onto the Afghan rug were too rumpled to tell her much, though she did make out the trousers from one of her father's suits. The handmade shoes were his, too. Even partly in shot the mahogany bed was also recognizable. But –

Her mother had never owned a pair of high-heeled silvered sandals like those.

But so what? All this snapshot indicated was that she'd been wrong – out of date – to think it still showed her parents' bedroom, instead of the place where her father and stepmother slept. Mere prejudice had made her get it wrong.

Except for one detail not in the picture. On it, rather, superimposed by the camera in faint red digits. The date when it was taken.

*

She hadn't the heart to let Josh see this. Later that day, helping make tea in Kitty's apartment, she waited until he was out of the room.

The photograph Miranda had found made it hard to speak to Kitty as gently as she wanted. Least of all when it came to the most important thing. She laid the adoption paper in front of Kitty. Who was surely braced for – what?

Kitty gave it just enough attention to know what it was. Her lack of response left Miranda uncertain whether to be amazed or not

Then she thought: of course. As she'd tidied and delved and blundered through Kitty's possessions, for months gone by this discovery was only to be expected. Maybe Kitty was surprised that it had taken Miranda so long.

'Kitty?'

She looked up at Miranda. Closely, with anxiety? Or with potential relief?

'Kitty – all these years. Why has this stayed a secret?'

She could guess why at first no one had known. It wasn't hard to imagine the young Kitty, back home in wartime England, sleepwalking through the rituals of secrecy dictated to unmarried mothers. Banished perhaps, to the semi-derelict house at Stumblehurst, where she could hide away in what the world then saw as unbearable shame.

'It shouldn't have been so terrible, should it? I mean, the illegitimacy thing. I'd never have kept quiet if it was no more than that.' Kitty's face was calm and candid; her hands though were shaking.

She added, 'Read any damn thing you find. I daresay someone else knowing about it will be a kind of exorcism. So long as you don't ask me anything more.' She glanced towards the kitchenette to check that Josh was still out of sight. 'You were going to ask something else, weren't you?'

Miranda passed her the photograph she'd found, with its giveaway date superimposed on the discarded clothes

– Adam's, Julie's – on the floor of the room where both her parents had still slept. This time, though Kitty still showed no surprise, her face did harshen. She too understood the meaning of what she saw. At that moment any stranger chancing on their shared look of anger might never have guessed they loved each other.

'Josh, darling,' Kitty said, as he came into the room with three mugs of tea, 'would you mind going to the shops? I'd like Mandy to go over some lists with me.'

After he'd left, Kitty handed the photo back.

'I'd left it where I found it. Among your mother's things. Maybe it was there by accident. Most likely they – probably the woman – it usually is – could have meant it to be discovered and stir up trouble.'

Trouble between Miranda's parents, she meant.

Kitty's voice was still controlled but her face was flushed. She got uneasily to her feet – 'No – no, I'm the only one who can find this' – and moved to the engulfing swivel chair from which she programmed all her light shows and graphic designs. Unlocking a desk drawer, she took out a video.

'I'm going to go and lie down, if you want to watch this. Just don't ask me to see any of it again.'

It was a home movie, of a kind. Just seeing the familiar room left her assaulted by a mob of emotions.

No mysteries now.

The identity of the couple on the bed... 'Oh, all right, you great dick...'

The view into a springtime garden whose cycle of flowering Miranda had known by heart from childhood.

Just by looking out of the window she could have told the date to within a few days.

But another vile detail declared the time of this scene. Everything was as in the precisely dated photograph she'd shown Kitty. But here, placed to make a point, was also a clock radio: the kind that confirms both the date and the hour. It stood at the edge of the picture on the stool from her mother's dressing table; in the foreground as a kind of subtitle.

See this, it said; see me? *This* is when. Now, watch ...

It was the week Miranda's mother was to die, seconds after leaving the motorway at twice the legal speed.

And then, right there in her parents' bedroom, the phone rang.

The worst was to come. She went on watching.

Forty-six

Part of her had always guessed that her mother had died betrayed. Even so, it was as if Laura had been killed twice over. All she could think of, in a rush of stupid, stupid pride – yes, okay, she knew – was how not to shed tears in front of anyone else. Tears of rage or compassion, never mind which. At the same time some other idiot part of her, running on automatic, still tried to jib at acknowledging a single frame of what she'd just seen.

Kitty came back in as Miranda switched off her computer. She must have been waiting for the chime it sounded when logging off.

These days she was walking, with a plastic crutch encircling her upper arm. Miranda stood up and took her other elbow to help her into a chair. Having watched what Kitty had asked her to, she was dizzy with rage: the floor could almost have shifted under her feet, as in an aircraft flexing its way through a turbulent sky.

Miranda held out the video. 'Tell me where you got this.' Anger made it hard to speak without slurring.

'It was in your mother's things. Someone had sent it to her on purpose. Afterwards Annie found it, in a pile of stuff she thought had better come to me.'

Their former cleaner, a good friend since Miranda could remember.

Kitty's face was closed down and pinched. There were tears in her eyes. It surprised Miranda that in all her aunt's life of secrets she'd never before seen her greatly moved.

It was Kitty who'd then been sending anonymous emails showing Adam and Julie in flagrante. Not with any plan in mind; just casting about, half out of her mind with rage and grief, for some gesture of revenge.

'Stupid, stupid, stupid! Unbelievable,' Kitty exclaimed. She'd taken off her glasses and was wiping her eyes, after several moments when she'd been unable to speak. 'For me to act so out of control.'

Miranda knelt down by her chair and embraced her. What else might she have done, in Kitty's place? It was something she'd rather not imagine.

Clinging to her, overcome by the wrongs done them both as well as to Laura, Miranda said, 'Dear Kitty, how can you possibly be to blame!' And wept with her after all.

*

So, going to see her father. He needn't think Miranda would keep quiet, even if he was still an invalid, kept in at St Edmund's for observation. Not now that Kitty had shown her everything she'd found out.

And Miranda was damned if she'd go home first and sleep on it. No way would that make a difference. Her, still nice and good? Forget it. When Frances' family had blown itself apart, Frances had tried to understand, and please everyone. So look where that got you.

On the Tube from Victoria Miranda dwelt on how the videos all of them – had got into Kitty's hands. She was still so angry, she stayed standing up when there were empty seats all down the carriage.

Throughout the time she'd been organizing her mother's funeral, other people were purging the family home of anything to do with Laura. The video had been there too in a pile of things – framed photographs of her parents' wedding, of her own christening, nursery-school paintings by her and Josh, love letters between her mother's adoptive parents during their dull yet hazardous wartime postings, the family albums – all put in bin liners and dumped in recycling crates as valueless. It was there, out in the front garden on rubbish-collection day, that Annie had found them, then taken it on herself to send them to Kitty.

Discovering all this, understanding struck Miranda as smartly as a blow to the head. So that was why Etta tried to keep her daughter out of hospital. She knew! All along, she'd known her children were mating with each other. It might be a solid talk show credential in the US; but here in England a public revelation like that wouldn't be at all useful to a rising politician. That was why Etta had been reluctant to call an ambulance; she'd guessed everything that Julie might say while anaesthetized.

Stamping up the escalator from the Tube, Miranda hardly noticed where she was. Nothing existed for now beyond the video sequence she'd seen that day. The one that

You Said She's Where?

had shown an ultimate boundary between Before and After.

In her parents' bedroom during the last hours of her mother's life, the phone had been connected up right through filming.

Not by accident: maybe Laura's call had been expected – hoped for, certainly. Naked, prone, being fucked by Julie as he spoke, in an ordinary, judicious-sounding voice Miranda's father gave a telephone performance that must have been the high of his life. The moment the receiver was down, they'd each come, then shrieked with mirth.

She got within sight of St Edmund's where her father was doubtless readying to reorganize his life. A busy existence, an important one, and in the long term as tidy as ever. His room was in the hospital's new wing, a high, curved construction like the world's biggest iceberg was bearing down on the street below. Looking up, all Miranda could think of was him taking the call from her mother. To get at him as he deserved she would have been ready to climb up the building's outside.

Her phone had failed, or she'd have called him already. Just to give him a suspicion of what she meant to say; enough to trouble him. Sod his recent condition.

Near the corridor entrance on his floor one of the staff came running after her.

*

Her father might still make a full recovery. Hearing this, Miranda didn't know what she felt. His crisis operation hadn't entailed heroic surgery but it had been extensive and fiddly. A rabble of emotions assaulted her, at odds with each other and every one unwelcome.

She came to the door number she been given. Went in.

The Frankenstein structure of drips and monitors was no surprise. But what of the other visitor there?

'Joshie?'

Her brother looked up. Long enough for both to see there was nothing much to say.

His face though. The whole look of him as he sat. Counter to all her fears and expectations he too was not here to triumph. Faced with the near-death of his father, had Josh recovered what she'd thought of as his magnanimous real self? They sat across from each other in silence beside the bed and its sheeted non-presence: not a living person whom neither respected, just an unconscious entity not expected to wake until long after. After a while Josh got up, saying where he would wait for her.

Feeling nothing – not yet – she lingered, crushed by an ocean-swell of fatigue. All the way here she'd been fired up and driven by uncomplicated anger. And now, unable to accuse her father to his face, she had no use for all that rage. The shock of her frustration was like being thrown against a wall.

She pictured the stages of her father's recovery; how prematurely thin and frail he'd be at first. No way would she stoop to shouting abuse at someone in that state; nor yet utter any well-thought-out denunciation in a quietened voice. The first chance she had, she'd be out of her one-time family home. Somewhere clear and away from him.

You Said She's Where?

By degrees she could see that, as with her bleeding and brutalized stepmother, she now had two relationships with the de-personalized figure in front of her. Adam had deserved to be an object of contempt; to ignore that would count as supping with a very short spoon indeed. Meanwhile he was no worse than any sick ageing patient; someone whose distress you'd care for without a thought.

It was a comfort that for now she could see him as just a collection of symptoms. For weeks to come it meant even her own hostility was something that couldn't get at her.

After a while she got up and left to go to the nearby pub with Josh.

Forty-seven

Having been more or less dropped by their father, for Miranda as well as Josh their past itself had seemed cancelled. But now she could see their life anew. Others were there who'd always cherished their existence: people for whom they'd been so much more than heartsore debris from times gone by. The evidence was everywhere – in the photo of the unknown Frenchman with a look of Josh in his face, and above all in the record of their lives made by Laura from behind the camera.

It also lived on in Kitty's allegiance, now declaring itself in a way no one had anticipated.

*

On the day Miranda went to see the Royal Academy's current show, there was one point where the crowd gathered, then moved more slowly than elsewhere. Next to Josh's exhibit a grid of video screens showed the rape of several forests, played backwards so that every tree rose again unharmed. On the other side was a film of the artist's penis being impaled. Compared with most works there, Josh's seven-foot-high painting, 'Self-Portrait with Terrorist', must have been seen as mainstream, even unadventurous. It was still a main attraction.

'You can tell it's an old person's work,' Miranda heard one woman say. Not the only onlooker mistaking Kitty's role in the painting.

What it showed was the naked likenesses of Kitty and Josh, posed together full-face as for a Victorian studio photograph. She sat, wearing the *médaille de la Résistance* on a string round her neck; he stood with one hand on the back of her chair. No detail of either body was hidden from public inspection.

Despite the picture's frankness, it wasn't about bodies. What it revealed was the match of two minds: the physical contrast was there to point up their shared inner likeness.

One that Miranda should have recognized sooner. Josh had resisted the theft of his life by Adam's replacement family, only to be branded as dodgy and sad. But Kitty, in time of war, had also tried to oppose an invader. Rightly – for the most part – the world had labelled her a heroine.

Don't ignore your wrongs, the painting said, just because everyone tells you anger equals bad form. Know your real friends, the ones with a sense of justice no matter what blunderers they themselves are. That way you'll also know yourself.

*

At home among Kitty's former possessions the diary lay waiting. Though not quite packed for her flight to the States, Miranda picked it up and began to read the last pages.

This book is printed on paper from sustainable sources managed under the Forest Stewardship Council (FSC) scheme.

It has been printed in the UK to reduce transportation miles and their impact upon the environment.

For every new title that Troubador publishes, we plant a tree to offset CO_2, partnering with the More Trees scheme.

For more about how Troubador offsets its environmental impact, see www.troubador.co.uk/sustainability-and-community